Shadow of His Hand

DAUGHTERS of the FAITH SERIES

Shadow of His Hand

A STORY BASED ON THE LIFE OF
HOLOCAUST SURVIVOR ANITA DITTMAN

Wendy Lawton

MOODY PUBLISHERS
CHICAGO

All Scripture quotations are taken from the *Holy Bible, New International Version®*. NIV®. Copyright © 1973, 1978, 1984 by International Bible Society. Used by permission of Zondervan Publishing House. All rights reserved.

Editor: Cessandra Dillon
Interior Design: Ragont Design
Cover Design: Barb Fisher, LeVan Fisher Design
Cover Photo: RM/Corbis—Anita Dittman

Library of Congress Cataloging-in-Publication Data
Lawton, Wendy.
   Shadow of His hand : a story based on the life of holocaust survivor Anita Dittman / by Wendy Lawton.
      p. cm. — (Daughters of faith series ; bk. 6)
   Summary: The daughter of a German and a Jew, Anna's dreams of becoming a famous ballerina are crushed by increasing Nazi persecution, but she is sustained, even while in a Nazi work camp, by her strong Christian faith and the conviction that she will one day be reunited with her mother and sister.
   ISBN: 978-0-8024-4074-7
   1. Dittman, Anita—Juvenile fiction. 2. Holocaust, Jewish (1939-1945)—Juvenile fiction. [1. Dittman, Anita—Fiction. 2. Holocaust, Jewish (1939-1945)—Fiction. 3. Jewish Christians—Fiction. 4. Christian life—Fiction. 5. Jews—Germany—History—1933-1945—Fiction. 6. Germany—History—1933-1945—Fiction.] I. Title.

PZ7.L4425Sh 2004
[Fic]—dc22

2004000279

We hope you enjoy this book from Moody Publishers. Our goal is to provide high-quality, thought-provoking books and products that connect truth to your real needs and challenges. For more information on other books and products written and produced from a biblical perspective, go to www.moodypublishers.com or write to:

Moody Publishers
820 N. LaSalle Boulevard
Chicago, IL 60610

5 7 9 10 8 6 4

Printed in the United States of America

For Anita

Contents

Acknowledgments

Special thanks to Anita Dittman who met me at a hotel in Minneapolis and let me interview her for hour after hour. She never shrinks from telling her story, no matter how painful. Thanks to Jan Markell who helped Anita write her autobiography, *Trapped in Hitler's Hell*. To many of my questions, Anita would say, "Look at the book. Jan described it exactly." That's high praise.

Lisa Abeler, women's ministry director at Camp Lebanon in Upsala, Minnesota, first told me about Anita and bought her autobiography as a gift for me. Lisa was sure Anita would be perfect as the subject for a Daughters of the Faith book. She was right. Thank you, Lisa.

And thanks to those who form the team—my editor, Michele Straubel; the others on the editorial/design team, Cessandra Dillon and designer Barbara LeVan Fisher; my agent and ally, Janet Kobobel Grant; and my longtime critique partners in SALT.

Look at Me

ook at me. Look at me!" The delicate curve of the girl's
arm continued through the arc of her two middle fingers
—a perfect ballet position. She pirouetted with a sense of
grace and balance rare in a five-year-old. Blonde braids flew
straight out as she turned. *"Vati,"* she said to her father,
"Look at me."

"Anita, stop showing off and quit making all that racket."
Her father turned to her mother. "Hilde, get that child out of
here." He sputtered in anger, his German words tumbling
over one another, "It's insult enough that you failed to give
me even one son, but must I put up with two tiresome girls
every waking hour?" He raised his hands toward the ceiling.
"Whatever possessed me to marry a Jew?"

"Fritz! Not in front of the children."

Anita stood frozen for a moment before she slipped into a
corner, squeezing herself in between the wall and the chest.
Her slender arm reached out to pull nearby Teddy onto her

lap. She hated it when her mother and father fought. Lately it happened all the time, but Anita never meant to start yet another argument.

"Hella, take your little sister out to the kitchen." *Mutti* used her hands to gently hurry them toward the door.

Anita hung back, wanting to be near her mother, but Hella gave her a sharp jerk that left no doubt about the outcome. Once in the kitchen, Anita leaned her face against the doorjamb.

"Anita tries so hard to please you. Can't you see that she only wants your approval?" Mutti's voice could be heard in the kitchen almost as clearly as if they stood in the same room. The Dittman row house, located in the Breslau suburb of Zimpel, was spacious and luxurious, but it had one drawback—angry voices penetrated the walls as if they were made of paper.

"Don't start with me, Hilde." Vati paced the floor. "I have my own difficulties and I don't need your complaints heaped on top of them."

"Trouble crowds in on all of us these days, Fritz, but can't we try to shield the girls as long as possible?"

"Hella does her best to please me—I have no problem with Hella, but Anita . . ."

Anita put her hands over her ears. Hella tried to pull her outside, but Anita scooted under the table, looking for refuge. Her stomach hurt.

"Why do you show such favoritism? Hella is ten years old. Of course she is more able to control herself." Mutti's voice tightened. "Anita may be tiny, but she is a bundle of energy and creativity. If you could just see her for herself and forget the boy you wished for . . ."

"I admit it—I wished for a boy. A lot of good that did. I shall discuss this no further." Vati slammed a hand down. The sound made Anita flinch. "Do you know what I really wish?"

Mutti did not answer.

"I wish I had never married you. Whatever was I thinking? Marrying a Jew—it's sheer madness for an Aryan!" Vati spoke each word with chilling precision. "Hitler is calling it 'race disgrace' now—the mixing of pure German blood with that of the Jew."

Mutti's quiet sobs carried to the kitchen.

"Let me tell you, Hilde, my wife," the words my wife dripped with sarcasm, "that one stupid act has caused me no end of grief."

Mutti still didn't answer, but her responses never mattered to Vati. Once he got going, he could argue for hours all by himself.

"Not that you care one whit about my trouble. Things are changing—that's a fact—and here I am, saddled with a Jewish wife and two half-breed daughters."

Anita heard the door slam.

"Anita, Hella, come in here, please." Mutti's voice sounded sad.

Hella took Anita's hand and pulled her out from under the table.

"Mutti, I'm sorry." Anita put her arms around her mother's leg. "I never meant to make Vati angry."

"Hush, Anita," Mutti said in that soothing voice. "Hush." She put an arm around Hella as well. "Your father worries about things and takes that worry out on us."

"Vati hates me." Anita's stomach still hurt.

"Don't be silly, Anita." Hella's voice rang with impatience. "Fathers do not hate their own children."

"Hella is right," Mutti said. "Vati's anger comes out in mean words, but that anger is not really directed at you, Anita." She smoothed the flyaway strands that escaped Anita's braids.

Anita didn't argue with Mutti, but she felt Vati's rejection whenever she tried to put her hand in his hand or when she tried to sit in his lap. He always found an excuse to pull away or shoo her off. She'd become an expert at watching his face for reactions. When Hella came near, he rarely pulled away.

"Why does Vati get so angry these days?" Hella sounded confused.

"It's complicated." Mutti stood up and moved across the room to straighten out the folds of the curtain. "It's politics and his job mostly."

"Politics?" Hella took Teddy off the floor and sat him on Anita's lap.

"You know about all the trouble brewing with Hitler's ideas, neh?" Mutti asked.

"Some."

"The newspaper Vati edited has been part of the movement they call the *Social Democrats*. Everyone expected things to get better after the financial chaos of the last few years, but here it is 1933 and Germany is more uneasy than ever."

Anita poked at Teddy's eye. She didn't understand what Mutti said. She wished they would talk about things that she knew.

"Hitler hates the Social Democrats, and Vati now must join the Nazi party or . . ."

"What's Nazi, Mutti?" Anita disliked the way the word

sounded. When people said it, they pulled their lips back and it made their faces look angry.

"It's not something you need worry about." Mutti came and playfully pulled on Anita's braids. "Your tiny head should be filled with ballet, pretty dresses, your fuzzy family of teddy bears, and—"

"You don't need to tell her that, Mutti." Hella lifted her hands in exasperation. "She cares for nothing but drawing and dancing anyway."

"And that, *Mein Liebling,* is how life should be for a five-and-a-half-year-old. Come, girls, and let's sit and talk while I turn edges on this chiffon ballet skirt for our littlest ballerina."

Anita pulled a long, deep breath in through her nose, picturing how fluttery the petals of chiffon would look when she twirled. Just like the storms she loved, her gray mood passed quickly and she once again resembled her aunts' nickname for her—Ray of Sunshine.

Teddy and his bear friends, along with pencils, drawing paper, and ballet continued to fill Anita's life. When Mutti knelt down after ballet lessons to remove Anita's ballet shoes, the little girl always cried. She never wanted to stop dancing. At night she slept with her well-worn ballet slippers tucked under her pillow and dreamed of a wooden stage ringed with lights. Though she was the smallest girl in her class, in her dream when the *danseur* lifted her high above her head, she towered over all the dancers on stage. The shimmering colors, the smell of chalk on the floor, the dust motes rising up from the gaslights, and the rhythmic sound of toe shoes making padded thuds and slaps against the boards made her dream seem more real than her waking hours.

It was mid-dream one night when she woke to a gentle shaking.

"Anita, *Mein Liebling,* wake up. It's Mutti."

She rolled over, trying to recapture the dream.

"Anita. Listen to Mutti." Her mother pulled her to a sitting position. "I must leave, but I will come to see you tomorrow."

Leave? Suddenly the dancers faded and Anita focused on her mother. "You cannot leave me, Mutti!" She reached arms around Mutti's neck and continued screaming the same phrase over and over.

"Anita, Anita. You are very nearly six years old. Please don't carry on so. You are breaking Mutti's heart."

"I've had enough of this." Vati came into the room. He sounded angry. "I want you out of my house, Hilde. I want you gone now."

"But my daughters—surely you do not want them?"

"It's not a matter of what I want. I am an Aryan and my daughters are half Aryan. Your Jew blood taints their veins and that's bad enough, but I'll not allow your Jew ideas to contaminate them any longer." He stood with his arms crossed across his chest and his feet planted wide apart—an immovable force.

"You may have the right under Hitler, Fritz, but what about what's right under heaven?" Mutti's voice resonated through the house and a sleepy Hella came into Anita's room.

"Don't call on heaven, Hilde." Vati's voice cracked.

"Surely even you are not hypocrite enough. You do not believe in the God of your people. You do not believe in the God of the heavens either. Admit it." He stood with his hands on his hips and his feet apart. "That modern religion of yours believes in a weak concoction of Buddha, Mohammed, Jesus, animal gods, even—I don't even know how many gods you have." Vati straightened his back. "I am proud to be an atheist. In fact, I'm a devout atheist—I do not believe in God. Period." When he said "God" he spat it out of the back of his throat, like it was a bitter mouthful. "Religion is for the weak and you, Hilde, are the weakest of all. You cannot even manage to embrace one religion and stick there. You need to create your own little crutch made up of a hodgepodge of deities."

"Fritz, my philosophy doesn't matter here." She looked at the two girls. Hella stood frozen. Anita wept. "Hella, take your little sister to the kitchen . . . please. I will be there to speak with you as soon as I am done speaking to your father."

Anita grabbed Teddy and took Hella's hand. Once in the kitchen, the shivering Anita crawled under the table again, listening. Hella pulled out a chair and sat down. Anita could see her sister's foot rubbing up and down the calf of her leg. That's what Hella always did when she was frightened.

"I want you out of here, Hilde, and that's the end of it." Father's voice carried all the way into the kitchen. "I hope to cover my Social Democrat activities by joining the Nazi party and turning over the newspaper to them." He made that harrumphing sound he made to cover embarrassment. "After all, what good are ideals when one's life is at stake?"

Mutti said something, but Anita couldn't make it out.

"I may get away with my past by trying to fade away during this confusing time, but I'll never get away with my continued 'race disgrace.'"

Anita didn't understand much of what Vati said. She only knew that Vati wanted Mutti to go away.

"Don't leave me, Mutti," she cried to herself.

"Hush, don't upset Vati." Hella said in a whisper. "Poor Vati; he must do it."

Anita put her fist in her mouth to stop the cries. Hella loved Vati above all else. Even though Anita understood little, she knew Vati loved Hella best and Hella returned that love with unquestioning loyalty.

Vati lived in their home, but he was a stranger to Anita— a stranger she longed to please, but never could.

"If I gave the girls to you, I would have to give you money for their care. I would have to get you an apartment." Vati coughed. "This argument tires me."

Mutti said something else, too low to hear.

"They can learn to take care of themselves. You spoil them. In fact, they can care for me." His voice got louder. "Girls, come."

Hella pulled Anita out from under the table and pushed her ahead into Anita's bedroom where Vati and Mutti were. Anita still clutched Teddy.

"Your mother must leave, but you will visit her . . ."

"No! Mutti, don't leave me."

Hella pulled her little sister's braid. "Stop it, Anita, stop it!" Hella moved to stand in front of Vati. "I will help you, Vati. I can cook."

Anita looked at Mutti's face in time to see her wince in

pain as she started to reach her hand toward Hella, but then quickly dropped it to her side.

"Don't leave me, Mutti," Anita whimpered, quieter now but no less determined.

"Anita." Her father squatted down in front of her. Anita had never seen him so close. He smelled of warm wool and shaving soap. "Stop crying and I'll give you a present." Vati pulled Teddy out of her arms and threw him on the bed. He reached down into his satchel and pulled out the large golden teddy with jointed arms and legs—the very one she'd longed for each time they passed the toyshop window. "Look . . . a nice new teddy."

Anita shook her head and pushed the bear away. She crawled up on the bed to retrieve Teddy. Without saying a word, she crawled back down and went over to Mutti and took her hand.

"Fine, then." Vati took the new bear and flung it across the room. "You win, Hilde. Take her and leave. Hella will stay with me."

Anita wanted Hella to take her hand, but Hella stood over by Vati. Her eyes didn't blink, but Anita saw her lips quiver.

"Hilde. Open up, Hilde. It's me, Inge." The knocking on the door woke Anita from a deep sleep. *Why is our neighbor, Inge, knocking at our door?* Rolling claps of thunder punctuated the banging on the door.

What a minute—Inge is no longer our neighbor. We left Vati last night. We're at Tante's house, not in our own house. She thought of her sister. *I wonder if Hella is sleeping in my bed at home?* The knocking grew more insistent. *Why is Vati's neighbor, Inge, knocking at Tante's house?* Anita shook Mutti, lying next to her on the cot. "Mutti, someone's knocking on the door for us. It's Inge."

Mutti stood up and wrapped a shawl over her nightdress. Anita stayed in bed, listening to the claps of thunder. She loved storms. Her mother often told her about the ferocious thunderstorm that raged the night she was born.

Drawing back the lock and opening the door, Mutti greeted her friend.

"Oh, Hilde. You must come." Inge's breath came out in uneven puffs as she grabbed her friend's arm with both of her hands. "You must come. Hurry." She took up much of the doorway with her soggy woolen cape.

Anita slipped out of bed to get a better look.

"What time is it? Come where?" Mutti wrapped the shawl tighter around her shoulders.

"It's in the early hours of the morning—perhaps two." Inge shivered.

"Forgive my manners. Come in. Catch your breath."

The younger woman stepped inside, but did not sit down. "You must come back to your house. When you left yesterday, Fritz left soon afterward. We didn't think anything about it, since he rarely stayed at home when you were there." She poked a wet strand of hair under her hood. "Tonight, when the storm broke, we heard banging sounds from inside the house and thought perhaps Fritz had returned."

Mutti began to wring her hands.

"When my Otto came home an hour ago, he heard the

knocking and banging sounds right through Fritz' door. As he went to the door to ask if all was well, Hella called out." Inge put her hands on her hips and shook her head. "Your Fritz had not yet been back since he left the night before—more than twenty-four hours earlier. The thunderstorm had terrified Hella, but the door was locked and she had no way to get help."

"Hella . . . oh, no. My Hella . . ." Mutti began to pull her clothes on over her bed clothes.

"She told me you were staying over here temporarily and asked if I would get you."

"Thank you, thank you." Mutti kissed her friend.

Without further conversation, a tired, wet Inge took her leave and hurried to go back home.

Mutti dressed Anita and the two of them followed, walking back to the only home Anita had ever known.

When they arrived, Mutti fitted her key into the lock and Hella practically fell out of the house into her mother's arms. Hella clung to Mutti, sobbing. Anita stood alongside, patting Hella's arm. As Mutti murmured comforting words, they gathered a few things and left.

As they walked down the silent street in the hour just before dawn, Hella let go of her mother's hand to shift her umbrella. "I should have left Vati a note." Her sobs had long since given way to sniffles. "Do you think he'll worry?"

❧   ❧   ❧   ❧

Days later when the three of them came back to pack their things for the move to the tiny apartment they'd found on the other side of Zimpel, Anita's stomach ached the whole time.

Hella slowly packed her things, carefully smoothing out all the wrinkles and lingering over every memento. Anita figured Hella could finish much faster if she wouldn't keep looking to the front room where Vati sat, shoulders hunched, listening to the *wireless*.

As they gathered things for the last parcel, Vati walked into the room and put a tentative hand on Mutti's arm. "I . . . well, I realized it wouldn't have worked out caring for Hella after all. Sorry."

Hella kept her head down and moved toward the door.

As they stood there watching the movers loading the last box on the truck, Vati looked hard at Mutti. "I agreed to give you and the girls money each month against my better judgment. I don't have to, by law, you know, because you are a Jew." His eyes narrowed and he lowered his voice to a whisper. "I think I've managed to make a clean break from my political past. You see before you a proud member of the Nazi Party." He paused and then spoke with precision, "If you so much as breathe a word about my past, Hilde Dittman, you'll not get another cent. Do you understand?"

Mutti just looked at him.

"*Auf Wiedersehen*, Vati." Hella ran and hugged him. "I love you."

Vati stood still, looking uncomfortable with his arms by his sides. As Hella moved away, Vati reached an awkward hand up to pat her head.

Anita stood nearby, wishing he'd say good-bye. *Look at me, Vati, Look at me.*

A Time
to Dance

Judenfratz." Anger spilled out of the boy's mouth along with the single word that meant Jew-brat.

The startled six-year-old Anita flinched and dropped her ballet satchel. One pink satin slipper tumbled out onto the street. "Mutti, what does that mean? Why is he mad at us?"

"Pick up your shoe and brush it off, *Mein Liebling.*" Mutti opened the satchel so Anita could put her things back in order. Mutti handed the bag back and waited until the boy left before speaking. "Some children have nothing better to do with their time than to bully helpless little girls."

"Shall we tell his mother?" Anita knew he lived near their apartment.

"Oh, no, child. No." Mutti shook her head, sighing. "You must be very careful with what you say. Things are topsy-turvy these days. I don't want to speak any further about this, but you must remember this—" Mutti paused in the street and squatted down right in front of her daughter. "Are you listening carefully?"

Her serious tone frightened Anita. "Yes, Mutti, I'm listening very carefully."

"No matter what anyone says or does, you must keep your head down and go on about your business. No matter what. Do you understand?"

"I think so."

"And when you are out on the street or even at school, do not make eye contact with anyone. Do you know what eye contact is?"

"No."

"It's when you look at someone eye to eye." Mutti stood up and looked over her shoulder as if only just aware of the attention her conversation with Anita might draw to them. "Come, let's walk. Always keep your head down and your eyes averted."

"But why? I don't understand. Is our new neighborhood dangerous?"

"No. Not any more than any other neighborhood in Germany. Let's talk tonight at dinner, neh?"

Mutti hurried her on to ballet practice. This would be the last practice before Anita's recital at Breslau's beautiful Century Hall.

How Anita wished she still fit her chiffon ballet costume, but she'd already outgrown it. The silky petals of the skirt had fluttered and quivered with every movement. There was no money to buy fabric for a new one. Her ballet slippers were worn shiny, and they fit so snug that it took Mutti a long time to work them onto Anita's feet.

"No matter," *Frau* Mueller-Lee, her dance teacher, had said. "You will capture every heart when you dance."

Her words always gave Anita hope. Less than a year ago, Frau Mueller-Lee had called Mutti to a meeting to talk about her daughter's future. Anita still remembered the meeting. Her teacher had looked at Anita and said, "Child, with your natural talent and my training, you will someday be famous. Audiences will worship the very stage you dance on." From then on, Anita spent two hours a day with Frau Mueller-Lee, doing calisthenics, etiquette, and her favorite—ballet.

Mutti sighed and put her lips together in that worried way of hers when Frau Mueller-Lee complimented the tiny dancer, but it was the stuff of Anita's dreams.

Now she was to dance her most important performance ever. Mutti found an old crepe paper costume that had been Hella's. The paper had faded slightly, but once carefully steamed, the pink and blue looked more delicate than ever. Anita didn't even ask for another chiffon costume. She knew Mutti had gone without coffee to scrape together pennies for some paper flowers to wreath her hair.

Anita sighed. Her shoes pinched her toes, but she vowed to dance her very best. The better the dance, the less it mattered that her costume was only made of paper. She practiced as diligently as if the studio were a stage.

That night, as the sisters set the table, Mutti seemed preoccupied. "We must talk about the events happening around us." She put a bowl of soup on the table with three slices of warm pumpernickel bread. "I long for you to have a gentle childhood, filled with friends and games and parties, but most of all, I wish it could be free of worry."

The girls took their places at the tiny table tucked into the corner of the warm kitchen as Mutti ladled thin soup into each bowl. Anita sensed Mutti's seriousness. Neither girl seemed to know how to reply.

"Sometimes it feels as if the world has gone crazy." Mutti sat down. "Hitler is working his way to complete power in our country. Hella, you understand this, neh?"

"*Ja*, Mutti."

"President von Hindenburg has long been unwell—weak. In his place Hitler managed to push his way in, using the unhappiness of the people to seize power. But, weak as von Hindenburg is, he's the one who stands between Hitler and his hatred for the Jews."

"Why are people unhappy?" Anita knew she was mostly happy.

"It's complicated, *Mein Liebling*. After we lost the World War, the German people took a beating. We had no money and precious little pride left. Adolf Hitler spoke to the German sense of pride. The message came at a time when people needed hope."

"So, he's good then?" Hella sounded confused.

"Oh, no. No. It is dangerous to say so, but Hitler is bad, very, very bad." Mutti put down her spoon, leaned forward, and looked at both girls. "You must listen to me very carefully and try to understand what I am saying. Our lives may depend on it."

Anita put down her spoon. "I will listen hard, Mutti."

"And I," Hella added.

"Day by day, Hitler's evil unfolds. Just this spring Parliament passed the Enabling Act. That law gave Hitler all the power he will ever need. You've seen me sitting here at the table listening to the *wireless*, neh?"

The girls nodded.

"Every day Hitler reveals a new part of his plan. Remember when we had to walk over to the district office to register?" Mutti continued, "We had to declare our nationality. Not German, mind you, but Aryan or Jew."

"What's Aryan?"

"Hitler decreed that it means a white—Caucasian—person who is not Jewish. When we registered, you girls registered as half Jewish, since your father is Aryan. I registered as a Jew."

"Is that bad, Mutti?" Anita asked. "You do not go to *synagogue*."

"Doesn't matter. Hitler hates the Jewish people. He also hates those who are poor or handicapped. *Ja,* and the Gypsy people and—"

"That's a lot of hate, isn't it?" Anita didn't know why, but her stomach ached. She broke off a corner of her bread and ate it slowly.

"Yes, little one. Too much hate. That's why we must talk. Every day sees more laws—Jews cannot own land; Jews cannot keep their seats in the symphony. Jews cannot exhibit art in the galleries; Jews are prohibited from being newspaper editors—"

"It's a good thing Vati is an Aryan." Hella took a deep breath in through her nostrils.

"*Ja,* but he has his own problems because of things he wrote in his newspaper over the years. For his sake, you must not mention him or talk about him, even to your friends."

The sisters nodded.

"This is the hard part." Mutti leaned in close and talked in a low voice. "We must be very careful what we say and do. The only place you may speak freely is at home. And—this is important—we must not repeat anything we hear at home to anyone."

"What about to our friends?" Hella shifted in her seat as she rubbed one foot against the other leg.

"How 'bout Frau Mueller-Lee or my teacher at school?" Anita wanted to ask a question, too.

"I'm glad you ask the questions," Mutti said. "You need to understand this. Our lives will depend on it." Mutti broke off a piece of bread. "You must not talk freely with friends or even with your teachers. You two may be the only students at your school who are not members of the *Hitler Youth* organization. You must be cautious; they will be allowed to say or do anything they like to Jewish students."

"So you mean we can't fight back, like when that boy called me *Judenfratz?*" Anita didn't like to be called names.

"*Ja.* That's right. You must look down and walk away. You must not talk back and you must not fight. Hitler's people listen everywhere."

"I don't understand," Hella said.

"As Hitler came to power, he brought his bodyguards with him—the *Schutzstaffel* or, as they are now called, the *SS*." Mutti shuddered. "They are to be feared." She put her head in her hands, shaking it back and forth. "Oh Hella and Anita, my sweet little daughters, I hate to tell you to live in fear, but if I keep from warning you in order to protect you from the ugliness, I might very well be sending you straight into the heart of trouble."

"We are big enough to understand, aren't we, Anita?" Hella came and put an arm around her mother. "We'll make it like our game—our secret game. Anything you say to us will be locked in our hearts."

"*Ja!* And nobody has the secret key 'cept Hella, Mutti, and me."

"Why did I worry about you girls? You are my wise ones." Mutti hugged them both. "And we will play the game together. Now—tell me the parts of the game."

"Everything we say to each other gets locked deep inside." Anita sat up straight, proud that hers was the first answer.

"We must not fight back if we are teased," Hella added.

"We need to keep our eyes down and our heads down when we are on the street." Anita smiled wide. "That was a hard one, wasn't it, Mutti?"

"And we mustn't ever talk about Vati," Hella said, "or he might get in trouble."

"Can we lift our heads to watch the brown shirts marching down the street in a parade?" Anita wondered who could ignore the explosive sound of hundreds of men goose-stepping down the street. It reminded her of the thunder she loved.

"No, no, no." Mutti pulled Anita close. "This is one of those confusing things. Those brown shirts are the *SA*—the storm troopers. They are much like the *SS*. Dangerous. They are all Nazis. They may be marching, but they are watching. Always watching." Mutti took Anita's face between her hands. "Hitler decreed that no Jew can salute the *Swastika* flag, so if you raised your arm in salute you could be taken away. But here's the hard part—if you are standing on the street when a parade turns the corner and you do not raise your arm and shout '*Heil* Hitler,' you can be slammed to the ground or even worse for the disrespect." Mutti planted a kiss on Anita's cheek and said, "Enough of this doom and gloom. Our soup may be lukewarm, but it's nourishing. Let's eat."

"But Mutti," Hella asked, "if we are on the street and the flag goes by, what do we do?"

"Slip into a shadow. Carefully and slowly make your way out of sight without drawing any attention to yourself."

The shadows will cover me. Anita liked that idea—another part of the game.

On the night of the recital, the city never looked prettier. Mutti, Hella, and Anita took the streetcar to the hall. They left home hours early to make sure nothing would go wrong. The lights sparkled, and the fragrance of summer jasmine scented the air.

Backstage, Mutti braided Anita's braids so tightly that the little dancer's scalp pulled. She imagined that her eyes must have stretched wider. Mutti then wound the braids into a figure eight at the nape of Anita's neck and pinned the paper flower wreath to her head.

"*Schön.* What a cunning little thing." The flutist stopped on her way to the orchestra pit. "How can a tiny child like that be dancing already?"

Anita smiled at the compliment. After all, *Schön* meant beautiful, but she couldn't bear to let the misunderstanding about her size stand uncorrected. "Thank you, *Fräulein*, but I am much older than I look. I've always been slight, but I dance like the big girls."

The musician laughed. "And how old are you?"

"I am six, nearly seven years old."

"Forgive me," she laughed again, "I hadn't realized how very old you are. I look forward to seeing your dance." She winked at Mutti as she left.

Anita drew herself up to her full height, trying to hold her head high in a classic ballet stance. The hunger to dance sometimes grew stronger than the hunger for food. "When she sees me dance," she said to Mutti, "I don't think she'll laugh or wink."

"Oh, Anita," Mutti said, "you are one of a kind. Sometimes I think you are the spitting image of your father—all the good things of course—along with a dose of that stubborn German pride."

"Do you think Vati will come tonight?" Anita asked as Hella came backstage.

Mutti did not answer.

"Eine Kleine Schwester," Hella said. "That costume looks *wunderbar*. Mutti, you did such a beautiful job."

Anita loved the compliment, but not being called "baby sister." "Hella, I'm big. I'm dancing with the biggest girls. None of the little dancers are performing tonight."

Hella laughed that beautiful rich laugh of hers. "Oops. I guess you are getting too big to be called 'little sister.' I shall be far more careful in the future."

"Places, dancers." Frau Mueller-Lee bustled through the troupe of nervous girls.

"Come, Hella." Mutti planted a quick kiss on Anita's rosy cheek. "Let's take our seats out front."

The sound of the orchestra tuning their instruments always stirred something inside Anita. It was the sound she hoped to hear for the rest of her life. She knew that Mutti thought her too young to know her future, but when she danced—whether practice at the *barre* or during a performance —Anita knew contentment. As her muscles stretched and her limbs reached, she felt happier than at any other time. Sometimes at night she'd dream of flying. Her earthbound body would lift off the floor and she'd soar. In real life, dancing felt like flying. The ache in her stomach went away, and her body seemed to float somewhere between earth and the heavens.

Her solo dance came near the end of the evening. As the older girl before her danced, Anita became so caught up with the fluid motions of the choreography, she nearly forgot her own dance. Then she listened to the applause and knew it signaled her turn.

Anita took a deep breath in through her nose and let it out slowly through her mouth. Frau Mueller-Lee told her that exhaling released every bit of nerves and allowed a performer to focus on the dance. She ran out to center stage, remembering to keep her toes pointed and her back straight. The leather on the bottom of her ballet slipper made a whispery brush-thud on the wooden stage as she ran. Starchy crepe paper rustled with every step. She couldn't see anything beyond the footlights. Mutti and Hella sat somewhere in the audience. Was Vati out there? *Look at me, everyone!*

The music seemed to carry her. Her dance welled up from deep inside her. She worried for a moment that Frau Mueller-Lee would be angry about the improvised steps, but the dance overtook Anita as her body moved to the music.

When the dance ended, she seemed to wake. The audience stood to their feet and clapped. She could only make out shapes, but the applause went on for the longest time. She put her hand to her lips and blew a pretend kiss toward where she imagined Mutti sitting. Anita couldn't wait to see her mother backstage.

"*Brava!*" Mutti hugged her daughter tight, crepe paper and all. "You danced your very best ever." She handed the excited dancer a rose. "If only money would allow an armful of roses, but there's time enough for that. This is from *Tante* Käte's garden."

"*Danke*, Mutti." Anita put her face into the petals and breathed the rose scent.

Hella laughed. "Hothouse roses don't have any smell, so our ballerina got the best rose after all."

Anita hugged Hella. She wished she could hug the whole of Breslau tonight.

Later, as they walked to the streetcar, Anita listened to the rustle of her crepe tutu under her coat. The stars were brighter and the air clearer than she could ever remember. "I just love Germany," she said, spreading her arms wide. "Aren't we the luckiest people in the world?"

Neither Mutti nor Hella answered.

The next morning, Mutti gave Hella a coin she had saved to buy a newspaper. The music and art editor had been at Century Hall last night.

Hella hardly got in the door before Anita took Teddy by the arms and began jumping up and down. "Read it, Mutti. Read it!"

Mutti opened the paper and ran her finger across the article until she came to a familiar name. She began to read, "The dance was beautifully performed by six-year-old Anita Dittman. Her skill and grace at ballet far exceed her years. Nevertheless, we Germans no longer wished to be entertained by a Jew." Mutti blinked as if suddenly struck across the face.

The very air seemed to go out of Anita and she looked smaller than ever. Before Mutti or Hella could reach out to her, Anita took Teddy and wedged herself into the shadows between the bookcase and the wall. Anita may have only been six, but she knew last night was her last performance.

Mutti and Hella came and sat near her on the floor.

"No one can take last night away from you, *Mein Liebling.*" Mutti ran the back of her fingers down Anita's cheek. "No one who attended will ever forget you. Hitler may have decreed that Jews cannot dance on German stages, but he cannot stop your dancing spirit."

Never Leave, Never Forsake

Anita played outdoors as often as she could. The three rooms of their apartment made for close quarters. When Vati had stopped sending money, they learned to get along on public assistance and whatever Mutti could earn.

When Hella asked why they no longer got letters from Vati, Mutti pressed her lips together. It wasn't until they took the streetcar to the house of *Oma*—Vati's mother—that the girls learned about Vati. *Oma* had asked Mutti to let the girls visit, but Mutti hated to send them all the way to south Breslau. When *Oma* finally sent the carfare, Mutti reluctantly agreed to let them go.

Oma looked older than they remembered, but she still stood ramrod straight and spoke her mind. "Your father will not send another penny to your mother after what she did." *Oma* looked over the top of her glasses at Hella and Anita as if they were the ones responsible for whatever Mutti supposedly did.

The girls sat quietly, never knowing when they should speak in their grandma's presence or when she expected them to keep still.

"You do know where your Vati is, don't you?" *Oma* poured hot chocolate from the delicate Bavarian pot into two matching china chocolate cups.

"No." Hella opened her napkin onto her lap. "We haven't heard from him."

"I don't doubt that. He's in prison."

"Prison?" Hella jumped up, letting the napkin slide to the floor. She grabbed her grandmother's arm. "Why, *Oma*? Why is Vati in prison? Is he all right? When will he be out?"

"You should ask your mother."

Anita saw the anger on her grandma's face. It reminded her of Vati, when he had made up his mind about something. "Mutti doesn't know anything about Vati. She hasn't heard from him."

"Your mother turned Fritz in to the authorities. She knows exactly where he is. One of the prison guards told your father it was your mother who gave evidence against him. That's what convinced your father to complete the divorce." *Oma* crossed her arms over her chest.

"No, *Oma*," Hella said. "Mutti would never do that. She even told us not to mention Vati for his own safety." Hella sat back down and managed to retrieve the napkin and put it back over her knees without ever taking her eyes off *Oma*.

Oma seemed to consider that possibility. "Perhaps it's a ploy of the Nazis to get your father to put aside his Jewish wife . . . but, no matter. What's done is done. Drink your chocolate. It's so very hard to get these days."

Anita looked at her chocolate. There was nothing she loved better, and she hadn't had it for such a long time, but . . . "Is Vati all right?"

"*Ja.* You know your father. That one will always land on his feet. He turned his newspaper over to the Nazis and they will need him to train the new people. I think once he's severed all ties to your mother, he'll be released."

Hella took a sip of chocolate, but she never said a word.

"When your father gets out, you can come to visit him here at my house once in a while." *Oma* poured herself a cup of chocolate and settled in to tell the girls about her cat, her aches, and her neighbors.

Anita listened without speaking. She knew Mutti hadn't turned Vati in, but she knew it wouldn't matter. The three of them would make it without his help, somehow.

One of the first things Mutti had done to help ease the burden was rent out one room to a German seamstress and the other to a working girl. That meant they had only one room for cooking, eating, and sleeping. That's why Anita played outdoors at every opportunity.

Even though she no longer danced or took calisthenics, her body remained lithe and athletic. She jumped rope longer, ran farther, and walked faster than most of her friends. When the sun shone, Anita played.

One afternoon she sat on the low fieldstone wall near their apartment, waiting for two of her school friends. Waiting always made her antsy, so she jumped up and began walking along the wall, pretending to be a tightrope walker like the Russian performer she once saw in a book.

"Get down, *Judenfratz*." A group of six girls came toward her.

Anita remembered what Mutti had told her. With her head down and eyes averted, she continued walking the wall.

"I said, get down!" The largest girl grabbed one of her braids and yanked hard, pulling her off the wall. The rough stone scraped the side of her leg as she fell.

These girls could not be ignored. When Anita looked up, she saw six girls, including her two friends. Both of them looked away.

"Stop sniveling, *Judenfratz*," the same girl shouted as she grabbed Anita. One of the Dittmans' neighbors turned the corner carrying a bag of groceries. When she saw Anita and her tormentors, the neighbor looked down at the street and crossed over to the other side.

The more Anita wriggled to get out of the girl's grasp, the more the bigger girl pummeled her. The others landed a few punches as well.

"There. That'll teach you to think you can play with Aryans. You need to keep to your own kind." The girl spat on the ground. "And don't think you can tell anyone. We are members of the *Hitler Youth*. If you tell, we'll have your mother arrested. We can do it, you know."

Anita didn't answer. She knew they could do it.

"Get up and clean yourself off. You look a mess." The girl laughed and all the others laughed with her. As they walked away, they continued to mock Anita and laugh.

She felt like staying right there, but she knew that she

must not draw attention to herself. *Teddy . . . I'll play with Teddy.* She stood up, brushed herself off, and went inside.

Not everyone practiced those kinds of cruelties. True, there were Nazi families all around the Dittman apartment, including the apartment right above, but there were others like Frau Schmidt and the Menzels.

Frau Schmidt wore a smile that seemed to crinkle her whole face. The best thing about her was that she always seemed to cook too much food. Many a night, she'd knock on the door after dark with a pot of noodles cradled between two potholders or a half-loaf of bread.

Mutti said that knowing German women like Frau Schmidt reminded her that all was not lost. "Remember Frau Schmidt, girls, when you are tempted to think all Germans agree with Hitler. They may not be able to disagree openly, but their small acts of kindness take as much bravery as outright rebellion."

The Menzels lived in their apartment building as well. All three of their children still played with Anita and Hella. They were Germans and Catholics, yet, despite the danger, they welcomed the Jewish Dittmans into their home and into their lives.

One Easter, Frau Menzel invited Anita to accompany the family to Mass. Anita already knew about Jesus and about Christians. Despite Hitler's campaign against religion, for some reason he'd not yet stopped religious instruction in school. Anita went to religion class every week and learned about God and Jesus, the Lutheran Church, and its beliefs.

Mutti didn't mind. She'd long since left the Jewish faith behind. When she and Vati were students, it became fashionable to either become an atheist like Vati—believing there was no God; or a theosophist like Mutti—believing there was a little bit of truth in all gods.

So Mutti didn't mind Anita joining the Menzels on Easter Sunday. "Tell me all about it when you come home, Anita," she said as she smoothed Anita's hair and tucked a strand back into her braid.

Gunther Menzel led the way as they walked to church. Anita's excitement made it hard for her to stay back with his two sisters, Ruth and Krista.

"Run up ahead, Anita," *Herr* Menzel said. "You and Gunther can join the procession first." Everyone knew that Anita's and Gunther's ages made them the closest playmates. Besides, as he often told Anita, she could run and jump and climb as good as any boy he knew.

"What's a procession?" It sounded like fun to Anita.

"You will love it," Gunther said. "The priest leads us into the church. He wears beautiful white vestments for Easter. After the Mass, he tells us about the passion."

"The passion?"

Frau Menzel said, "It's the story of Jesus' life, death, and resurrection. When you go into the church, look at the stained glass windows. Each one tells part of the story of Jesus' life. You will see."

"I love stories," Anita said as she skipped alongside Gunther.

Gunther hadn't told her about the music. As they joined the march into the church, the sound of the organ swelled and the notes seemed to vibrate in Anita's chest. Many people held candles. Incense mixed with candle wax scented the whole church. It felt like another world to Anita.

Before they took their seats, the Menzels kneeled. Anita couldn't help but compare the quiet act of kneeling, head bowed, to the defiant "*Heil* Hitler" that filled every courtyard.

As the Mass began, many of the words confused Anita.

"It's Latin," whispered Gunther.

When the priest began telling about Jesus' life, Anita understood. Like Frau Menzel suggested, Anita followed the story in the stained glass windows as the priest talked. With the sun shining through the vividly colored glass, the images in the window seemed alive. Some of the glass pieces were cut like prisms and sent rainbows across the pews. The church building and Anita's friends seemed to fade as she heard the words and saw the outstretched hands of the Messiah. Just as the notes of the organ penetrated her very chest, the Jesus of the stained glass windows seemed to come right into her heart.

When the priest read a verse that said that the Heavenly Father would never leave nor forsake, Anita somehow knew that He was her Father. For the first time, she felt protected and understood. She looked at Jesus' hands in the window of the Resurrection. *I know those hands better than I know Vati's hands. Jesus will protect me*. She knew it.

On the way home, the skip disappeared from Anita's step. Not that she wasn't happy; it was just that she was so full, all she could manage was to deeply breathe in the air. She felt such peace.

"Anita, did you enjoy the Mass?" Mutti arranged three boiled eggs on the table. Both women who rented rooms had gone to their families for Easter.

"Oh, Mutti . . ." Anita paused, trying to find words. "As I listened to the sermon and stared at the beautiful windows, the Jesus of the story came right out of the window and into my heart."

"Mutti, don't let her talk such silly things," Hella said. "Her imagination seems to grow as fast as she grows."

"It happened." Anita knew it didn't actually happen. The window was made of glass and lead. She knew the Jesus depicted on the window did not come into her heart, but she also knew it happened in some other way. "I can't explain it."

"Religion is often filled with mystery," Mutti said.

"But it's not about religion. I don't know how to say it." Anita searched her mind for words. "I don't have the words, but I know something happened."

"You have such a gift for imagination, Anita. I'm sure you do believe something happened." Mutti handed each of the girls a little gift. "Ours is probably the only Jewish home celebrating Easter, but Frau Schmidt sent these little lithograph chicks for you."

The chicks were embossed on a piece of cardboard in bright shiny color. Anita turned the piece over to see the reverse embossing on the dull side of the card. What a day this had been.

Later that night, as she lay in bed next to Hella, she leaned over the side where Teddy lay. "Look Teddy, did you see this Easter chick? I had a wonderful Easter." She reached down and rubbed Teddy's mended paw pad. "Not just because of the gift—I met Jesus today. Mutti and Hella don't believe it, but I know it's true." She left the chick card in Teddy's lap and lay back on the bed. *Yes, I now have a Father who will never leave me nor forsake me.*

4

Peace
amid Chaos

utti," Hella came into the room, excitement in her voice. "I found out today that if Anita can pass the entrance exams she can attend Bethany tuition free!"

"No," said Mutti, "surely that can't be true." She shook her head. "Your father agreed to pay for your tuition, but I did not dare to ask him for Anita's."

Anita could hardly breathe. She hated school. Mutti had managed to scrape together enough money to pay the fee so Anita could attend public school, but because she was the only non-Aryan in her class, teachers took pleasure in ridiculing her before the entire class. As each year passed, school had become more and more unbearable. When Gunther still attended, he'd meet her in the yard on many days and tease her out of her despair. Now, at age ten, she'd finally finished primary school.

"I've been so worried about where to send Anita for middle school. Do you think it's true, Hella?"

"*Ja,* Mutti. They gave me this note to bring home. It tells when Anita may take the exams."

Exams. Anita's mouth went dry and her stomach tightened.

"One of my friends has a sister Anita's age. I'll borrow her books over the weekend and Anita can study." Hella turned to her sister, "You can do it. I know you can."

Her words gave Anita hope. If only she could do it. The thought of attending a school that welcomed Jews and refused to enforce the Nazi regimen seemed too good to be true.

In the years since Hitler came to power, each day brought fresh troubles to the Jews as well as to anyone who hesitated to follow the Nazi dictates. Anita remembered the day news of President von Hindenburg's death had come over the *wireless.* Mutti used to talk about the aged president as the only shield between Hitler and the Jews. When the president died in 1934, all possible opposition to Hitler died with him. As Mutti heard the news, she leaned over the table, laid her head on her arms, and wept. Hella sat next to Mutti, rubbing her back and murmuring the same kind of words Mutti had used to comfort them when they were little.

Now Anita went into her corner with Teddy and prayed a phrase she had heard at Mass. "Cover us with the shadow of Your hand, Father." She loved the thought of curling into her corner, covered with the hand of God.

Each new crisis seemed to be followed by a period of relative calm. Anita often wondered how life could go on despite all the upheaval, but it did. Some days they almost forgot the doom that hung over the land. When Anita heard she passed the exams and had full scholarship to Bethany Lutheran School, she had to keep herself from dancing down the street.

"Get all your homework done today." Mutti tidied the room while Anita and Hella lay across the bed studying. "We're going to take the streetcar into Breslau and go to church tomorrow."

"Church?" Both girls said the same word at the same time. Hella's question held an overtone of disbelief.

"Yes, church." Mutti began dusting the wooden wardrobe. "We'll attend St. Barbara's. I've heard through some Jewish friends that the pastor—I believe his name is Pastor Hornig—has a heart for Jewish people and works with an organization that secures visas and passports for Jews."

Disappointment swept over Anita for a moment. At first she thought Mutti had decided to go to church to find God, not just to find help escaping. *What does it matter? I'll get to go to church whatever the reason!* Anita looked forward to tomorrow.

"Are we going to try to leave Germany?" Hella sounded frightened.

"*Ja.* If we can, we will." Mutti shook her head. "I know we have no money, but I understand this organization helps pay for the relocation as well."

"But what about Vati? Would we leave him?" Hella asked.

"Now that he is a Nazi and remarried to an Aryan, he's in no danger, Hella. The situation here in Germany worsens every day. I'm sensing that war clouds gather. Nazi troops are even now marching into Austria."

"But surely we are safe," Hella argued. "Because you married an Aryan and because you are not a religious Jew, you'll not be troubled, right? And we are half Aryan."

"So far it seems that way, but the situation changes every day. There may come a time when Hitler will decide we, too, are Jewish enough for his wrath. What if that time comes when it is too late to leave?"

Anita closed her book and reached for Teddy. She might already be ten years old, but she still loved Teddy. She had other bears—her newer Steiff, Petzie, and a tiny one named Pimmie—but Teddy was the one she loved. His joints were loose and Mutti had patched his felt paw pads more than once. His fur had practically worn off in spots, but he had the kindest face. Something about him still comforted her when things went topsy-turvy. The thought of leaving Germany made her stomach ache.

The next morning they woke early and took the streetcar before most of Breslau even stirred. They got off at the closest stop and walked the last few blocks to St. Barbara's Lutheran Church.

"What a pretty church." Anita loved the old stone church on sight with its tall bell tower and steep roofs. The interior nearly took her breath away. The vaulted ceilings soared high above the stone floor. Sunlight streamed in through the arched windows.

"You are right, Anita. This is a beautiful church." Mutti spoke in a hushed voice.

The singing, the readings, the sermon—all made Anita feel as if she'd finally come home. She looked at Mutti to see her listening closely. Hella sat quietly, but Anita could see that her attention wandered.

After the service, the pastor came up to meet them. "Welcome. I'm Pastor Ernst Hornig."

"I am Hilde Dittman and these are my daughters, Hella and Anita. I am a Jew, though my husband is not." Mutti waited for a reaction.

"You are most welcome at St. Barbara's. The Lord seems to be sending many of His people our way." Pastor Hornig laughed. "We are delighted that He trusts us with His chosen ones."

Anita knew already she liked this man. The way he bent over as he talked to his people reminded her of the stained glass window at the Menzels' church showing Jesus feeding His followers. Maybe that was why Pastor Hornig seemed familiar.

Mutti spoke with him about passports and visas, and he promised to come visit them soon so they could talk at length.

And he was as good as his word. He came to visit—not once, but many times. He began the work to get them documentation to leave Germany and things looked promising. In the course of his visits, Anita found out that he and his wife had six children. He liked to talk about his family and the church, but, even more, he liked to talk about the Lord.

"Do you know the Lord, Anita?" Mutti and Hella hadn't yet come home, and as he waited for Mutti, he visited with Anita.

She told him the story of the windows. "Jesus came into my heart that day, but I don't know very much about Him."

"Well, it's a good thing I brought presents today," he

said. He handed her a package wrapped in brown paper and twine. "Open it."

Anita unwrapped the package. It had been a long time since she had received a present. Inside were three new Bibles. "For me?"

"Not all of them." He laughed. "One for you, one for your mother, and one for Hella. Do you like my gift?"

Anita ran her hands across the binding. "I do. Ever so much! I will read it every day."

"I not only want you to read it, I want you to try to memorize parts of it. We never know when we may find ourselves without a Bible."

Mutti and Hella walked in.

"Look! Pastor Hornig brought us each a Bible."

Mutti took hers. "How can we ever thank you for all you do? The more I've come to know you, the more I realize the sacrifice you make for us and for other Jews. Not just financially, though I know these Bibles cannot have been inexpensive." Mutti opened hers. "You know the risk you take for yourself and for your family by befriending Jews, neh?"

"Of course I know. I'm already *blacklisted*, but the Lord continues to shield me. God does not call us to an easy faith. Too many in the church have given over and allowed Hitler to commandeer their pulpits." Pastor Hornig shook his head. "I'm not alone. There are several of us. We call ourselves the Confessing Church and are committed to following Christ no matter the cost."

"I first came to your church because of the possibility of getting help to flee Germany . . . and I appreciate all the help you've offered." Mutti sat down across from the pastor.

"What I found was far more valuable. I found a faith I could finally trust."

Pastor Hornig tilted his head and waited for her to go on.

"At first I watched you, wondering why you did what you did, but it wasn't long until I saw that you always pointed us to Jesus. I realized you couldn't do what you do without Him. I want that kind of faith as well."

Anita hadn't moved, but those were the words she had longed to hear. She looked to see if Hella felt the same way, but she was busying herself with the hot water kettle.

"Hilde, all you have to do is to confess your sin and ask the Savior to cleanse you of that sin. He will do the rest."

And Mutti did, right then and there.

Church became the center of their lives. Despite the worsening political climate and impending war, Anita felt a peace like she'd never felt before. Mutti seemed to feel the same.

Attending school at Bethany became another bright spot. Deaconesses taught the classes. They were kind and fair and didn't seem to notice whether a student was an Aryan or a Jew. Not a single "*Heil* Hitler" could be heard in the school and none of the students belonged to the *Hitler Youth* organization. For the first time in her life, Anita worried about things like clothes, sports, and friends. Bethany Lutheran School remained an island of calm in a sea of chaos. For some reason, Hitler had not yet closed the *parochial* schools, though he'd announced his intention to do so. Anita guessed he just hadn't gotten around to it yet.

One day Anita stayed late at school. As she walked home alone, she saw someone running toward her in the distance. It looked like Hella. As the figure grew closer, Anita's stomach clenched. Panic lined Hella's face.

"Quick, come." Hella grabbed Anita's hand. "Mutti's been arrested."

Mutti arrested? How can that be? Anita ran. She no longer cared about drawing attention to herself. How would she live without Mutti?

When they reached the apartment, Anita couldn't believe it. Every drawer was open with its contents dumped on the floor. "What were they looking for?"

"I don't know. According to Frau Schmidt, the *Gestapo* came. At first they searched for something incriminating, but when they found nothing, they accused Mutti of 'race disgrace.'" Hella sat down on the floor in the middle of the mess. "Frau Schmidt said that someone told the Nazis that Vati had been with Mutti last night. Aryans must not 'fraternize' with Jews—it's now a crime."

Anita automatically reached for Teddy. "But we haven't seen Vati. It's a lie!"

"That's the sad part. Charges do not need to be true."

"What will happen to Mutti?"

"I don't know. If the charges are dismissed, she may be home tonight." Hella left it at that, but Anita understood how big an "if" it was.

The girls set about cleaning the apartment and putting everything to rights. Their boarders had long since moved out since it was now dangerous for a German to be living with a Jewish family. That meant that the girls could talk freely. When everything in the room had been tidied, there was nothing to do but wait. The sound of the clock ticking reminded them that the night slipped away.

Anita prayed as she waited. She repeated the verse from Isaiah she'd first heard at Mass with Gunther. Pastor Hornig considered it a promise for the Jews: *I have put my words in your mouth and covered you with the shadow of my hand—I who set the heavens in place, who laid the foundations of the earth, and who say to Zion, "You are my people."* She repeated that verse many times as she waited.

Finally, when it seemed too late to hope for a release, they heard the soft sound of footsteps in the hall outside the door.

"Mutti!" Both girls grabbed her at the same time.

"Let me come inside, girls." She looked exhausted. "This time I was released from these false charges, but I've been *blacklisted*. I will be watched from now on." She sighed. "In fact, we will all be watched."

Hella poured Mutti a cup of the drink they called coffee—it was actually made of grain, but it was hot and it was soothing.

"Let's pray and thank God for my freedom, even if temporary." Mutti bowed her head and began to pray. ". . . and Lord, speed the paperwork for our escape from Germany before it's too late." Rather than let that petition stand, however, she added, "Not my will, however, but Thine be done. Amen."

Anita nearly nodded off during the prayer, but she silently added her thanks . . . *and continue to keep us safe under the shadow of Your hand.*

5

Shattered Fragments

"Hilde."

Anita heard the name whispered outside the door, followed by a barely audible knock. "Come in," she said. She recognized the voice of their friend.

Frau Schmidt quickly stepped inside the door. Her hair stood up as if she'd been running her hand through it. She looked past Anita and spoke directly to Mutti. "They are burning the *synagogues* and smashing the windows of any businesses still left in Jewish hands." Her chest seemed to deflate as she hunched over as if to protect her heart. "*Mein Gott*. May He protect His children throughout this night."

"Thank you for telling us, Frau Schmidt. I'll turn on the *wireless*." Mutti put an arm around her friend. "You must leave. It is far too dangerous for you to be here. If anyone suspects you of aiding a Jew, the punishment will be swift."

"How can Christians stand by? You do know I'd hide you if it came to that."

"You must not say things like that. You take enormous risks. Hitler's ears and eyes are everywhere, including our own building." Mutti wrung her hands together. "They brag that Breslau is one of the most Nazi cities in all of Germany. You must be careful."

"Don't go out. Don't let the girls go to school. Ever since your *blacklisting*, I worry about you." Frau Schmidt kissed Mutti and slipped out the door.

As their neighbor took her leave, Hella turned on the *wireless*. As she moved the dial, the eerie woo-ee noises, screeches, and static increased and decreased until Mutti found a station broadcasting a strong signal.

". . . and this will be a night to remember. Some are already calling it *Kristallnacht*—the night of broken glass. Apparently, tonight's action was a well-coordinated attack by the Nazis all across Germany in retaliation of the assassination of the German ambassador to Paris, Ernst vom Rath, by a Jewish youth."

The report went on, sounding more like the spirited account of a sporting match than the unfolding of a night of horror.

"Frau Schmidt is right," Mutti said. "We must stay put. Hella, you peek out the curtains to see what is happening around us. Be careful not to move them in case we are being watched."

The *wireless* alternated between news reports and Nazi patriotic music. ". . . Jews are being taken for questioning throughout the country . . ."

"Mutti, can we pray? I'm frightened. Not just for us, but

for everyone." Anita held her stomach and tried to get the shaking to stop.

"Can we please stop talking about God?" Hella put her hands over her ears. "Our world is falling apart. If God really existed, how could He let this happen?"

"Dear God in heaven," Mutti prayed, "we are frightened, we are sad, and we are filled with doubts. Touch each of our hearts. Calm us and care for us. Be with the people of Germany—those facing death and those trying to face their fears."

During Mutti's prayer, Anita's tears began to fall. At first her tears were for all those who faced the Nazis tonight. Soon her tears were for her own fears and loss. She could hear Hella crying as well.

". . . thank You for those who reach out to help us, like Frau Schmidt, Pastor Hornig, and the Menzels. Protect us, protect them, and rid our land of this evil scourge. Amen."

When the prayer finished and Anita's tears stopped, she felt refreshed somehow. Her hands no longer trembled.

They settled in for a long night of waiting.

The waiting stretched into five days before the siege ended. During those days, the hours were punctuated by the smell of smoke and the sounds of shattering glass, the percussion of heavy boots running in the street, fists pounding against doors, and sobbing—always sobbing.

Once the sirens finally stopped, word began to filter in from the Jews around them. Many family members had been herded up and taken away. Old men were pulled out of their houses by their beards, right in front of their families.

The hate messages continued on the *wireless*. The announcers boasted that soon Germany would be *Judenrein*—completely free of Jews.

"How will they do that, Mutti?" Anita couldn't figure out where all the Jews would go. Would Hitler allow them all to escape to England?

"You've heard talk of concentration camps, neh?" Mutti asked.

"Yes."

"That's how they begin. It seems to be a moving and a gathering and more moving—as to the final solution Hitler proposes, we don't know."

Anita hated moving. She still remembered when they had to move from their house to this tiny apartment. It turned her world upside down.

"The newspaper publishes fresh reports every day declaring certain towns and cities to be *Judenrein*." Mutti sighed. "I wonder how much longer until Hella is back with the mail. How I pray that our passports and visas are here."

Hella reported back. No visas and passports in the mail. Pastor Hornig had assured Mutti that the documentation could come at any time. When visas came, he promised, St. Barbara's would help with the cost of travel and relocation.

The letter that did arrive was not the one they were expecting. Mutti was out when the notice came, so it sat on the table until she returned. Anita and Hella were both home from school. Anita kept opening her book to begin homework, but the letter on the table felt like an evil presence in the room. Without even looking close, she could tell it came from the *Gestapo*.

What could it mean? Was it about Vati? Surely if they decided to pick up Mutti, the *SS* would show up at the door with the order in hand. Was it about her? Hella? She closed her book again. There was no sense in trying to do geometry. Without thinking, she reached over and pulled her tattered Teddy onto her lap. Burying her face in his fur, she inhaled the scent of childhood. She even imagined the faint smell of resin from the floor at Madam's studio. How life had changed. She guessed it was about to change yet again.

"Why the long faces?" Mutti came in and put her things on a chair. "Did something happen at school?"

"*Nein*, Mutti." Hella pointed to the letter on the table.

Mutti picked up the envelope. Her breathing grew rapid and the color drained from her cheeks. With trembling hands, she opened the envelope and read aloud: "Frau Dittman. You must leave your apartment in Zimpel to relocate to a residence in a Jewish neighborhood at 1298 Van Duesen Street where lodgings have been secured for you and your family. You have twenty days to comply with this order."

And so it begins. Anita remembered Mutti talking about the movement of Jews. This was step number one—the ghetto. Gather all the Jews together.

"I know this address," Mutti said. "It's right in the Breslau inner city."

"Will we take the streetcar to Bethany?" Hella asked.

"As long as it stays open. It's been nearly a year since Hitler promised to close the *parochial* schools. But for now they are still open. We'll figure out a way to get the carfare."

"We may be far from school," Anita said, "but we'll be within walking distance of church." She hated the thought of moving, but the letter could have brought much worse news. The *Gestapo's* official *blacklist* still contained the name Hilde Dittman.

"*Ja,* that's right," Mutti said. "We will save carfare on Sundays. Now we might even be able to attend church mid-week."

Anita looked at Hella. She rarely smiled anymore. Maybe it was because she was seventeen and almost done with child-hood. They used to pretend how things would be when they grew up—dancing, boyfriends, travel, a huge circle of friends. None of that came true. Now they must move from their tiny Zimple apartment to an even tinier flat in a drafty, rat-infested *brownstone.*

"Hella, are you okay?" Mutti looked hard at her older daughter.

"I don't know how many more changes I can endure." Hella sounded worn out. "You and Anita have your faith, which seems to help steady you." She ran a hand through her long hair. "I'm like Vati. I cannot bear that religious stuff."

"That's true of many people," Mutti said. "All you need do is give it a fair try and ask God to show you the truth. Keep your skepticism. He'll answer your honest doubts. The Lord knows what a skeptic I was when I found Him."

Hella rubbed the top of her foot against the calf of her leg. "When should we begin to pack?"

"We'll have to sell most of our things this time." Mutti said the words quietly. She knew the girls had given up so much already.

"Oh, Mutti . . . no. This is the last we had of our life with Vati." Hella ran her hand down the front of a polished wooden wardrobe.

"It cannot be helped. We have no money to pay for movers. Besides it's better we get the money from selling our things than the *Gestapo*."

Mutti didn't explain why she thought the *Gestapo* might get their things, but Anita knew she was thinking one step ahead.

"Hella, you must sell your books. You may take your clothes and a few personal things." Mutti put an arm around Hella. "I know it's hard, but there are families much worse off. Think of all our friends who've not yet heard about their loved ones taken on *Kristallnacht*."

Mutti often talked of those "worse off." When they were younger, the girls used to roll their eyes at Mutti's words. Now they knew the truth of them. Not that it helped much when facing another loss of their own.

"Anita, you are practically grown now—twelve years old. I will let you bring your new bear, Petzie, and your tiny Pimmie, but you must get rid of Teddy."

Anita couldn't speak. *Teddy? Why Teddy?*

"He's so worn, I cannot patch his paw pads one more time. The joints are loose, and it's just a matter of time before he's in shreds. If he wasn't so big, I'd let you keep him for sentimental reasons, but he is nearly as large as a small child. No matter how much I wish it were different, we simply will not have room."

Anita wrapped her arms across her stomach. Mutti had given up so much and Hella had to part with her books—

what could Anita say? She avoided looking at the bed where Teddy rested. "May I wait until the last day?"

Mutti put an arm around Anita. *"Ja."*

As they sold their furniture and family treasures, Anita felt that sense of loss again. She kept telling herself that they were just things and that people were more important, but she couldn't help grieving as each familiar piece went out the door. She looked over at Teddy. He seemed to represent everything about her childhood. And soon he'd be gone as well.

Stop it, Anita. They are only things. Most of the families around you are mourning the loss of people. How can you fuss over furniture and a tattered Teddy? After all, poverty was nothing new to the Dittmans. Ever since Vati had left, Mutti and the girls lived from day to day. Were it not for the kindnesses shown to them by neighbors and by Pastor Hornig, they often would have gone hungry. Anita's stomach growled constantly, but since many of her classmates shared her problem, they'd learned to laugh at the chorus of stomach noises.

One night, a few days before they were set to vacate the apartment, Mutti opened the door to a tentative knock. Anita looked up expecting to see one of their neighbors, but instead, standing not more than three-and-a-half-feet high, waited a thread peddler—a dwarf. She wore tatters and had the gaunt look of starvation.

"Come in, come in," Mutti said, leading the tired woman to the last chair in the house. "Would you care for a bowl of soup?"

Hella looked up from the floor where she sat doing homework. From the look on her face, Anita could see that she couldn't believe Mutti was offering food. They'd each only eaten a half-bowl of soup tonight in order to save a half-bowl for tomorrow.

"Thank you. Are you sure you have enough?" The woman's eyebrows lifted and she seemed to breathe in the lingering smell of the soup.

"Yes, it was left over from our dinner." Mutti turned to Anita. "Please heat up a big bowl of soup for our guest."

Anita got up to obey her mother, but she couldn't help wondering what they'd do for food tomorrow. With the move to the ghetto at the end of the week, they would need every bit of their strength. Besides, in the waning days of December, the wind blew bitterly. Anita had noticed that the less food you ate, the harder it was to stay warm.

"Now please, show me your thread." Mutti waited while the woman laid out six spools of thread. "I'd like that spool of cotton thread." Mutti handed her the five pennies for the spool and still the girls said nothing.

After the peddler ate and collected her thread back into her satchel, Mutti opened a drawer. "I have a pair of gloves I'm not going to be able to take on our move." She took out her only pair of gloves and gave it to the woman. "Can you use these?"

"*Ja.* God bless you." The woman's voice trembled. "God bless you all."

Mutti let her out the door and turned around to face her daughters. "Don't say it. I know we have nothing to spare. The only ones Hitler hates more than the Jews are people like her. Anyone who is special—handicapped or deformed in any way—will feel the full weight of Nazi hatred."

Mutti joined Hella on the floor and extended her arm for Anita to join them. "When I opened the door and saw her standing there, I felt compelled to offer help. This may sound strange, especially to you, my little Hella, but I felt as if God told me to feed and care for her. The Bible verse that kept going through my mind was the one that says, 'I was hungry and you gave me something to eat, I was thirsty and you gave me something to drink, I was a stranger and you invited me in.'"

Hella sighed. "I wish I could believe like you and Anita do, but all I know is that times are hard and I get so frightened about whether or not there'll be a next meal."

Anita didn't say anything. Like Mutti, she believed in God—but like Hella, she worried. *Is there something wrong with my faith?*

"I'm new at trying to hear the voice of God," Mutti said. "Maybe it was nothing more than my own pity. But we'll know soon." She playfully pulled on one of Anita's braids. "If it was the Lord who instructed me to offer it, He will replace what we've given away and then some."

It didn't take long to find out. The next day Frau Schmidt came over with food—a pot of savory soup, fresh baked bread still warm from the oven, and fruit. How long had it been since they had had fruit? The food would last for several meals. After Mutti thanked her friend, she raised her eyes toward the ceiling in silent thanks.

The next day someone came to look over the last of the things in the apartment. He offered a fair price for the lot; but when he came to the little chair on which the peddler had sat, he offered twice what it was worth. Mutti smiled as the man counted out the money into her hand. After he left she said, "I've had my answer. How about the two of you?"

Hella just smiled and shook her head, as if to question Mutti's mental state.

Mutti smiled. "I'm grateful because I'm convinced that over the next months, or even years, we will have to rely on God's provision and on His protection more and more. Whenever I'm tempted to question God's hand on our lives, I will think back to this day."

As their last day in Zimpel dawned, Anita knew she had one last task left to do. Before anyone awoke, she picked up Teddy and carried him down the stairs to the basement. Mutti was right; Teddy was too tattered to sell. In fact, he was too far gone to give away. But he always had the kindest face and despite the wear, his gentle expression never changed. Anita gave herself a little shake. It didn't matter. He would have to wait on the rag heap in the basement until the ragman came.

As she settled him onto the pile, Anita remembered the story of Abraham and the sacrifice of his son, Isaac. She wished God would provide a substitute for Teddy as he had for Isaac, but she knew she was being silly. To mourn over an old plaything when people all around her were being discarded seemed somehow sinful.

As she walked toward the stairs, she looked back and saw that familiar face looking back at her. He'd been her comfort and her confidant. *Good-bye, Teddy. I will never forget you.*

6

Auf Wiedersehen

"Hella, aren't you amazed that no matter how drastically life changes, we always seem to fall back into a routine?" Anita sat next to her sister on the streetcar coming home from school.

"I know. Sometimes I think a person could get used to anything. It reminds me of frogs. If you were to put a frog in a pot of boiling water, he'd hop right out."

"Eeuuw. What an awful thought."

"I'm making a point, silly." Hella shook her head—a movement she managed more often these days. At seventeen she was considered a real beauty. She wore her hair parted to the side in a long shiny bob, and when she shook her head, it drew attention every time. "Do you want to hear or not?"

"Sorry."

"If you put a frog in a pot of cool water and slowly heat it, the temperature rises slowly and the frog doesn't realize he's in hot water until he's boiled."

Anita made a face.

"Sometimes I think we're like frogs. As long as our trouble is cranked up one little bit at a time, we'll sit contentedly in the pot." Anita gathered her books together.

"This is our stop, so I think I'll hop out here." Anita smiled at her frog reference, but Hella didn't catch it.

Their old apartment had been crowded, especially when the boarders lived there, but this tiny apartment in an old *brownstone* gave new meaning to the word *cramped*. Four families lived in each apartment in the two-hundred-year-old building. In the Dittman apartment they shared their space with three other families, not to mention hundreds—perhaps thousands—of bedbugs. The cracks in the windows let in all kinds of other flying insects. Anita didn't even want to think about the vermin that lurked deep in cubbyholes and cabinets.

When she and Hella walked in the door of their room that afternoon, they knew something had happened. Mutti sat at the table with an envelope in her hands, turning it over and over.

"It's our visa, right?" Anita could feel the excitement bubbling up inside her.

"Not exactly." Mutti sighed. "We've been waiting on these papers for more than a year. Pastor Hornig worked on this at every opportunity before the Nazis burned the Help Organization."

"I know," Hella said, as she piled her books in the corner. The Dittmans had reapplied after they lost the Help Organization.

"It's been harder and harder to wait," Mutti said, "especially with war threatening." By late 1938 no one questioned that the country moved toward war. Marked Blackouts happened regularly now—these were practice drills in preparation for attack. The authorities ordered all lights turned off in the city so potential night bombers couldn't find targets. Everyone installed black shades in their windows and had to keep lights off during the drill. During Blackout the darkness was so complete that people had to wear fluorescent pins outdoors so they wouldn't bump into one another.

Mutti opened the letter to show the girls. Papers had come, but they were for Hella only. Mutti felt inside the envelope as if to see if she'd missed anything. "At least Hella has her documents." She tried to sound matter-of-fact, but Anita could see the tightening of her jaw. "Surely ours will come in the next few days. We must make plans for Hella to leave and we will follow her the moment our papers arrive."

"No!" Hella looked stricken.

"At first," Mutti said, "I couldn't bear to think of the three of us separated, but the more I considered it, the more convinced I became that Hella must go to England."

"Oh, Mutti . . ." Anita's stomach clenched.

"I know it will be hard to part, even if for a short time, but we mustn't turn down this opportunity." Mutti folded her arms across her chest in that way that always meant she'd made her decision.

As Hella prepared to leave, Mutti and Anita waited for their papers.

Soon after Mutti's decision, Anita came home from school with more bad news. Hitler had finally closed the *parochial* schools. With no advance notice, that day had been her last at Bethany. The good-byes had come hard. Bethany had sheltered its students in the midst of upheaval. Anita had no idea if she could continue her schooling. Where would they find money for tuition?

Like so many things in Germany, it was out of their control.

"We'll cover Anita's tuition at public school." Pastor Hornig caught Mutti after church to tell her. "I wish we could scrape together enough for books, but perhaps she can borrow them from someone."

"You are too kind, Pastor. You do so much for others; I worry about your own family."

"The family shares my anguish for our persecuted friends. Don't you be worrying, Hilde. It fills me with joy to see you growing in your faith." Pastor Hornig smiled. He and his fellow pastors—Dietrich Bonhoeffer and others—remained in what they called the Confessing Church. They refused to knuckle under to Nazi oppression and they came under increasing scrutiny. Pastor Hornig knew he was *blacklisted*, but he also believed God would sort it all out.

So Anita started yet another school. Since she'd last been to public school, the persecution of non-Aryans intensified. Students and teachers alike took great delight in mocking the Jewish students. It didn't help that Anita fell so far behind the other students. Without books, she relied on trying to remember what the teacher said. She took notes as well, but she discovered that some things were only found in the books—the teachers never mentioned them in class and yet often put them on the exams.

It wasn't long until Anita dropped out of school. There was little chance of learning without books, and it became dif-

ficult to put up with the bullying and the physical torment.
Besides, she wanted to spend time with Hella before she left.
How Anita hated the thought of yet another good-bye.

But the day came for Hella to leave. True to his word,
Pastor Hornig and the people at the Help Organization provided her with money and introductions to the people who
would help her in England. Mutti and Anita walked with her
to the train station.

"It cannot be much longer until our papers come. Pastor
Hornig assures me they've been sent." Mutti took Hella's
hand and kissed it. "The separation will be short—surely it
will."

Hella said nothing. She kept blinking her eyes. The situation inside Germany was volatile. Anything could happen.
Here it was—August 31, 1939—the end of summer. Who
knew what the winter would bring?

As they stood at the station waiting for the train, Anita
put her arm around her older sister's waist. "Don't worry
about us. Always remember how many times God covered us
with His hand of protection. No matter what happens . . ."
Anita couldn't finish her thought and the train whistle kept
her from trying.

As Hella stepped onto the train, Anita reached out one
last time to touch her fingertips. "*Auf Wiedersehen,* dear sister. May God keep you in the shadow of His hand."

Mutti could not hold back the tears. As the train pulled
out of the station, Mutti asked, "Why do I feel as if I shall
never see her again?"

Mutti and Anita's hopes of joining Hella ended just three days after Hella's train pulled out of Breslau. On September third, England and France declared war on Germany and all the borders were sealed. Escape was no longer possible.

"I'm glad Hella got out," Mutti would often say to Anita in the days following. "The Lord knows what He is doing, neh? Perhaps because of your faith, He knew you would be better able to weather the gathering storm. Ever since you were a child, storms never fazed you."

Soon after Hella left, three of Mutti's sisters, *Tante* Käte, *Tante* Friede, and *Tante* Elsbeth, moved into the cramped quarters with Mutti and Anita. They did their best to respect each other's space, but with so many people in such a tiny space, they practically tripped over each other.

Mutti and Anita walked to church by themselves on Sundays since Mutti's sisters were religious Jews. Sometimes the mother and daughter barely spoke, reveling in the quiet and the space.

Pastor Hornig always greeted everyone at the door of the church. He tried to keep up on everyone in his congregation. He wanted the church to be the safe haven in the storm. "Anita, I've learned of a Christian woman, Frau Michaelis, in Berlin who's willing to take you in. She's German, but her husband is Jewish. He escaped to Shanghai and her two sons to England." He put a hand on her shoulder, "I know your apartment is crowded. And since you left school . . ." He didn't finish his train of thought as he shook hands with one of the older men of the congregation. As the man went inside to take a seat, the pastor continued, "Frau Michaelis longs for a child to keep her company . . . her apartment is spacious and she agreed to pay for your schooling and books. I think Berlin will be safer for you. Outside the ghetto, you know."

Anita looked at Mutti, but her mother didn't say anything.

"You go in and sit down," Pastor Hornig said. "After you've thought about it and prayed about it, let me know."

They decided Anita should go, even though it meant another painful good-bye. Anita had feared that her mother might be arrested and unable to get word to her, but in the end they admitted that it could happen with Anita in Breslau just as easily. In spite of having made the decision, Anita's feeling of uneasiness persisted. Why would a German take the risk of inviting a Jewish girl into her home? It didn't make sense.

As Anita boarded the train to Berlin, she tried to memorize her mother's face. Would she ever see Mutti again?

My life is one good-bye after another. She thought of Vati and Hella. *I wonder what Hella is doing in England?* Her letters, smuggled in through a Dutch friend of Pastor Hornig, told of Hella studying for a nursing career. Vati had remarried and wrote on occasion, but mostly, he had moved on. So many friends left behind—Frau Mueller-Lee, Frau Schmidt, Gunther . . . the list seemed too long to recount. And now, Mutti . . .

Mutti stood with her on the train platform, wringing her hands. "I'm so thankful to see you out of the ghetto, but how I shall miss my ray of sunshine." Mutti took Anita's hands in hers. "When loneliness threatens, I will think of you going to

a wonderful school, eating healthy food, and keeping a generous Christian lady company."

Anita couldn't speak. She put her head on Mutti's shoulder.

"We will be together again. I know we will. You must not
worry about me. Remember the verse Pastor Hornig always
repeats from Isaiah 51: 'I have put my words in your mouth
and covered you with the shadow of my hand—I who set the
heavens in place, who laid the foundations of the earth, and
who say to Zion, You are my people.'" Mutti took Anita's
shoulders and gently moved her back, looking at her face as if
to memorize it. "When you start fretting, you just picture me
sitting under the shadow of the Lord's hand."

The train whistle blew. All the smoke and noise cut off
any further conversation.

"Write, Mutti. Tell me everything."

"I will, *Mein Liebling*, I will. You write as well."

"*Auf Wiedersehen*, Mutti." Anita held her hand to her
mouth and blew a pretend kiss to her mother out the window
of the train as the chugging sound increased. Mutti grew
smaller and smaller as the train pulled out.

When she arrived in Berlin, Frau Michaelis' tailor met her
at the train station. *How odd*. He seemed a nice enough man—
nervous, but friendly.

"This," he said to his employer when they arrived at the
upscale townhouse, "is Anita Dittman."

"Fräulein Dittman, this is Frau Michaelis." The tailor
opened his palm toward an older woman seated in the middle
of a horsehair sofa. Anita had never seen such a large woman.
There would not be enough room on either side of Frau

Michaelis to seat a small child. *Strange. Since the war, everyone seems to grow so thin. Things must be different in Berlin.*

"Welcome, Anita; put your things upstairs." The woman looked at Anita's worn suitcase and made a tsk-tsk sound. "You did bring your ration card, didn't you?"

"Yes, Frau Michaelis." Anita dug in her satchel and presented it to the woman. In wartime Germany, each person only got the food specified on the ration card. No matter how much money one had, one could only buy their limited ration. Food production always suffered during war. When farmers became soldiers, who grew the food? And Hitler believed the soldiers must be fed first—the people could share whatever remained.

Frau Michaelis hoisted herself off the couch and took the ration card with her into the kitchen, turning it over as she walked away, seeming to forget Anita.

"I'll show you to your room." The tailor led the way upstairs. "Frau Michaelis is a generous woman. She loves beautiful clothing, but because of her size, her clothes are hand tailored."

"You make her clothing?"

"Yes. She gives me a room in her home in exchange for my sewing."

"And she's been lonely since her husband and sons left?" Anita knew how lonely she'd been since she said good-bye to Mutti.

"Lonely? I don't know anything about that." He seemed to dismiss the subject. "Here is your room."

After the Dittmans' crowded room in the ghetto, Anita savored the space. How she wished Mutti could have shared the room with her.

At the first meal, rations were scanty. Anita figured they hadn't had time to shop for her rations yet. She appreciated them giving her a little of their food, even though her stomach growled long into the night.

She started school the next day. As she left, the maid handed her a delicate cucumber sandwich to put into her satchel. By the time lunch came along, she could have eaten a whole stack of sandwiches. How she hoped the maid stood in line for rations today, so she could have more food for dinner.

"May I sit here?" The girl speaking was a pretty teenager just about Anita's age. "I'm Ruth Conrad. You're new, aren't you?"

"Hello. Yes, I'm Anita Dittman. I just moved here from Breslau."

"Would you like a little piece of my cheese? Your sandwich looked awfully small."

"*Danke.* I'd love some cheese if you have any to spare." She took the little piece broken off the edge and put it into her mouth. It tasted wonderful. "I'm staying with a nice lady who must have decided when she saw how small I am that I eat equally small portions." She smiled. "In truth, I have the appetite of a half-starved wolf."

Ruth laughed. "You'd certainly be considered the runt of the litter."

"No fair," Anita said. She loved Ruth's teasing attitude. Perhaps she'd finally found a school friend.

"So, where do you live?"

"I'm staying with Frau Michaelis. Do you know her?"

"Oh." Ruth's face seemed to lose some of the fun. "Yes, she goes to my church."

"You go to church? Are you a Christian?"

"*Ja*. All the way. You?"

"Me, too. I'm half Jewish—my mother's a Jew—but I am one hundred percent Christian."

"I like the way you put that, Anita Dittman." Ruth's smile widened. "I prayed that the Lord would send me a fellow believer as a friend this year. Look at you! It's the first day of school, and He delivered you all the way from Breslau just for me."

"I can tell I'm going to like you, Ruth."

And that started Anita's days at her Berlin school. Her Jewishness seemed less important at this school than back in Breslau.

True to her word, Frau Michaelis provided all the books and the tuition. Anita surprised herself—she was a good student and she enjoyed every minute of school. Well, every minute except lunch. Her rations continued to be so small that Anita lost weight.

Ruth worried about her. "You need to tell Frau Michaelis to give you more food."

"I could never!" Anita opened her eyes wide at the thought. She and her benefactor barely talked. Frau Michaelis kept to herself mostly. She kept their relationship cool, almost formal. Anita wondered about the woman telling Pastor Hornig that she longed for company. He must have mixed her up with someone else.

Anita missed Mutti terribly. No matter how good school was, at night she cried herself to sleep. Was Mutti still safe? What happened in Breslau? Had they stepped up persecution of those on the *blacklist?*

Whenever Anita received a letter from Mutti, she read it over and over. Anita's letters were frequent as well. She made sure never to mention her hunger or Frau Michaelis' coldness. Mutti had enough to worry about.

"My mother sent this piece of bread for you." Ruth handed Anita a half slice of rich, dark pumpernickel.

"You cannot spare this, Ruth." Anita loved her friend's generosity. "Yours is a big family and each morsel of food is precious these days. I cannot accept that."

"My mother insists. When I told her that you'd grown so thin your skirts had to be pinned, she worried. But when I told her much of your beautiful hair is falling out, she said that can be a sign of severe malnutrition."

"We all lose weight these days . . ."

"Anita, don't you see? Frau Michaelis lacks for nothing money can buy. Money alone cannot buy food these days— you need money plus a ration card."

"What are you saying?"

"My mother knows Frau Michaelis from church. She seems a pious woman, but as one gets to know her . . . I don't want to repeat gossip."

Anita's stomach growled again and Ruth pressed the piece of bread into her hands. "My mother believes Frau Michaelis took you in order to use much of your rations for her own table."

"That couldn't be. She's been generous with tuition money."

"Which is worth more these days, Anita, food or money?"

"I wish I could talk to Mutti."

"Why don't you write and tell her about your hair and your weight loss?"

"Oh, I couldn't!" Anita couldn't imagine worrying Mutti. She had her hands full trying to care for her aging sisters and staying one step ahead of the *Gestapo*.

"Consider one question: How much weight has Mrs. Michaelis lost since you came?" Ruth finished her piece of bread and refolded the napkin it came in.

As Anita nibbled on the sweet, heavy bread, she remembered that the tailor had a stack of dresses to let out. *Oh, Mutti, I want to go home . . .*

That night the British bombardment started. It's not like the Germans hadn't anticipated the attack—the Nazis had made the mistake of bombing a quiet neighborhood in London. Notices had been posted throughout Berlin to be prepared for the English to bomb Berlin in retaliation—but the reality exceeded their worst expectations. As the air raid sirens went off, Anita and the rest of the household felt their way down into the building's basement. This was no easy task since the city was blacked out. Residents were not even allowed to light a candle out of doors. As a hodgepodge of people huddled together in the shelter, it sounded like the rumble of crashing thunderstorms above. Children whimpered, babies cried, and Anita prayed. Each time the bombing would go on for what seemed like hours. When the night sky finally quieted, Berliners received the all-clear signal and everyone made their way back to their apartments.

Frau Michaelis had a difficult time making it up and down the stairs. She had become even crankier since the bombardment started.

Anita wondered if Mutti heard about the bombing. The Nazis posted all news and notices on a wide pole in the ghetto. It became their link to news. Too often, however, the authorities withheld more information than they posted. Mutti probably still pictured Anita living in luxurious safe surroundings with good food and a generous benefactor. How Anita longed to tell her the truth. *I want to go home to Mutti.*

7
Erased from the Earth

The bombing continued. In Berlin, many thousands of people died. The sounds of screaming sirens followed by buzzing planes and the percussion of bombs took their toll on the citizens.

Weakened by malnutrition, Anita fell ill. Frau Michaelis —always overly worried about *contagion*—decreed that no one could go in or come out of Anita's room. The maid pushed a bowl of soggy cereal through the door twice a day, but Anita saw no one and talked to no one. Her homesickness grew intense. She longed to touch the soft skin on Mutti's face. She might be thirteen years old already, but she wished she still had Teddy. The silence and the loneliness ached worse than the illness. *What if I die all alone?*

But she didn't die. Her fever broke after several days, and she finally returned to school again. This time however, her homesickness continued. Anita longed to see Mutti. Sadness hung over everything she did. At least her studies took time and kept her mind off her family for part of each day.

Since the bombing continued nonstop, plans were made to evacuate the students to the Bavarian Alps. Anita wrote to Mutti to get permission to go. Now the coming "holiday" from the war was the favorite topic of everyone's conversation at school.

"Oh, Anita, will we ever have fun!" Ruth said as they walked along the school hallway and talked about what they would pack. "Just think—to be away from all this war, war, war for a time!"

"Do you think we'll finally feel like teenagers?" Anita loved that term. She'd come across it in her reading. She read at every opportunity—especially novels with fun-loving teenage characters living peaceful lives. What a difference from her experience. Nothing about her life had been normal since Vati left. Nothing.

"I will miss my parents, but the constant bombardment leaves me feeling jittery and nervous." Ruth's hands shook much of the time these days and she often jumped at loud noises. "I think my parents will relax if they know I'm safely out of the way."

"That's how my mother felt about me coming to Berlin." Anita laughed. "If Mutti only knew . . ." Anita censored her own mail much more strenuously than the *Gestapo* would. No sense in worrying Mutti. "I must admit, when we leave for the Alps, I'll not miss Frau Michaelis. I know I should be thankful, but—"

"Anita Dittman?" The school principal stepped out of the office and interrupted the girls.

"*Ja.*"

"A mistake has been made. I know we asked you to secure your mother's permission to evacuate, but . . . um . . . you will not be traveling with us after all." Without saying another word, he turned back into the office. At the door, he paused and turned once again to Anita. "Please leave your books in the outer office so another child can use them. It's a shame to waste them."

Just like that. Soldiers used the word *shell-shocked* to describe the emptiness she felt. She knew it would hurt later, but she couldn't react now.

Ruth looked stricken.

"I'm no longer surprised by things like these." Anita hugged her friend. "I will miss you, dear friend, but don't let it upset your trip. You need the vacation from trouble . . ." Anita gave her friend a playful punch. "So don't borrow my trouble."

Ruth couldn't speak. She had no experience with rejection. Seeing it acted out in the hallway left her stunned.

There would be no time for proper good-byes. Ruth had to hurry home, get her things, and meet all her classmates at the train station. All except Anita, that is.

"*Auf Wiedersehen,* Ruth." Anita said as she dropped her books off and started home. "I will never forget you."

As Anita walked home, her throat grew tight and her eyes stung. *Lord, You said You would shadow me with Your hand. Is this what You call protection? Is there nowhere for me?*

As she walked, she thought about the Lord. Ever since she first met Him in those stained glass windows, she knew He loved her. She understood that deep inside. *OK, Anita, don't despair now. Try to think of this in a new way.* She prayed that God would let her see the situation from His point of view. *Maybe God is not taking something away from me. Could He be moving me to something better?*

Her gnawing hunger made it hard for her to think. *Could God be closing the school door in order to open a door somewhere else?*

But what is the next step? She couldn't decide what to do. All she could think about was home and Mutti.

The farther she walked, the more she thought of Pastor Hornig. He also loved her and wanted the best for her. He believed she was safe and happy at Frau Michaelis' home—as safe as anyone could be in war-torn Germany. Anita longed to talk to him—to get his advice. By the time she made it to Frau Michaelis' apartment, she felt an overwhelming urge to call Pastor Hornig.

Without even thinking to ask permission, she picked up the big black phone in the hallway. She'd never once used Frau Michaelis' phone. But now she dialed the church phone number.

"Hello, St. Barbara's." The familiar voice caused tears to finally well up in her eyes.

"Pastor Hornig? It's Anita."

"Anita! What a surprise. I just visited your mother yesterday and we talked about the wonderful opportunity you've had to study and—"

Anita's tears turned into great hiccupping sobs.

"Anita, child, what's wrong?"

"Oh, Pastor." She could hardly get the words out. "I cannot join my classmates as they evacuate. They leave tonight without me . . . constant bombing . . . hungry. I'm hungry. . . ."

"Slow down. Tell me again. You've been suspended from school?"

"Y—yes."

"And you're hungry and frightened, right?" He paused as if to think of the right words. "Anita, everyone is hungry right now. The war affects us all." He paused to listen to the sounds of her despair. "Anita, I'll pray that the Lord will ease your burden, but you are safe in Berlin."

"You don't understand, Pastor. I've lost weight and my hair is falling out. My friend says I suffer from severe malnutrition."

"Why didn't you tell us earlier?" He sounded very upset and his sense of urgency changed. "I'll gather together the money to wire you a train ticket. You can tell me everything when you arrive home. It sounds like there's much I don't know."

So Anita came back to Breslau.

At the train station, Pastor Hornig took her by the shoulders and held her away from him as if he wanted to have a good look at her. He just kept shaking his head. "I wish you had told us, Anita."

When he brought her to her mother, Mutti kept running her hand over Anita's now-wispy hair and muttering something under her breath.

Mutti only saw the changes in her daughter, but Anita saw Breslau with fresh eyes. Homecoming highlighted how much things continued to change. The apartment seemed tinier than ever, the aunts more frail, and the bedbugs more vicious, but it didn't matter. Anita was home. She and Mutti vowed to stay together as long as they could.

"Mutti, where are Susie and Renate Ephraim? I haven't seen them since I returned. And I haven't seen *Herr* Levi, either." Anita almost hated to ask, but she wondered if any more friends were able to get out of Germany.

Mutti's face told the story. "Gone. Just gone."

"What is happening? Where will it end?"

"I wish I could answer that. At first we thought Hitler would be satisfied with taking our jobs, our homes, and our money. Then we began to hear the Nazis clamoring for *Judenrein*—Jewish-free cities. One by one we Jews registered, and then they began to round us up and gather us into ghettos like this." Mutti breathed deeply as if she were inhaling red-hot pain.

"And it isn't enough?" Anita knew the answer. Several men had been taken to a concentration camp called Auschwitz. For some reason, a few were released back to their families, but the stories that came back with them were too chilling to be believed.

"So we keep getting relocated and concentrated into smaller and smaller locations. It's beginning to look as if Hitler cannot rest until we are removed entirely." Mutti rubbed her hands over her face. "You know what the Polish *Gauleiter*, Hans Frank, said, don't you?"

"No." Anita knew that the *gauleiters* were Hitler's provincial governors, but she didn't keep up with things like Mutti did.

"He said, 'I ask nothing of the Jews except that they should disappear.'"

"Oh, Mutti..."

"Last month in Hitler's paper, *Der Stürmer,* they announced that 'Judgment has begun and will only reach its conclusion, when'... Now, how did that go?" Mutti thought for a moment. "... 'will only reach its conclusion when every knowledge of the Jews has been erased from the earth.'"

"Someone will stop Hitler, won't they?" Anita couldn't believe such hatred would be allowed to go unchecked. She wished Germany would open its eyes and see what was happening. *Look at us, look at us.*

Tante Käte couldn't stop feeding Anita since she had returned from Berlin. The five of them—Mutti, Anita, and the three aunts—shared precious little food, but every time they sat down to a meal, *Tante* Käte fished tiny bits of meat out of the soup to put in Anita's bowl. "I'm old and don't eat as much. This girl's skin is draped over nothing but bones. Eat. Eat." She laughed, "God forbid I should lose a few pounds."

All three of the aunts were much older than Mutti. *Tante* Friede and *Tante* Elsbeth seemed frail and tottery to Anita. Had they aged that much in a year? Anita loved all her aunts even though tight quarters meant that tempers sometimes erupted. They forgave as quickly as they snipped and snapped. All five of them worked hard to keep despair at bay. *Tante* Elsbeth would often start a sentence with "It could be worse..." Anita loved the way she tried to keep their spirits up.

Tante Käte was the youngest of the three. She was the artist and managed to bring some of her pencils and paints with her. She and Anita often sat huddled together, drawing. For Hella's birthday, Anita drew a self-portrait using only a small mirror. Mutti planned to smuggle it to Hella through their contact in Holland. *Tante* Käte never gave praise lavishly, but as she held the portrait and studied it, she said, "Anita takes after me. She vill be the artist vhen I am gone."

Tante Elsbeth took the portrait and studied it. "It could be worse than for our Anita to be cooped up in here with a fine artist who spends hours with her young apprentice."

Anita had pretty much given up on her education. Hitler's ever-worsening decrees tossed Jewish children from school to school until they used up all their possibilities. Every week Pastor Hornig asked Anita if she'd been able to enroll in school. Anita knew he worried, but she also knew that finding money for tuition was impossible.

One day, when the pastor came to visit them at home, he handed her an envelope. "Here is tuition for one year of high school." The high school, König Wilhelm Gymnasium, apparently still accepted Jews. "Someone anonymously donated your tuition."

Mutti looked at Pastor Hornig. "How can we ever thank you?"

Anita knew that Mutti believed the pastor himself had used his own money. It's no wonder so many Jews began following Jesus at St. Barbara's. The pastor loved his people sacrificially. When Ernst Hornig talked about Jesus' love and death on the cross, the people in the pews recognized that kind of love. They watched a daily example of that kind of selfless love being offered by their pastor.

So, once again, Anita enrolled in school. Hatred for the

Jews had escalated since Anita last attended school in Breslau, but she managed to ignore the *anti-Semitic* posters hung all over school. She carefully avoided the many potential pitfalls by reading signs and making herself as small and inconspicuous as possible. Before she even began school, she walked the campus to see all the prohibitions. Jews must not sit here, stand there, eat in this room, study at that table—she figured if she paid attention, she'd have less problems.

As she tried to curl into her chair in class, she laughed to herself. What a difference from the six-year-old Anita who longed to dance on the famous stages of Europe and whose favorite words were "Look at me."

Home became her haven once again. When she came home from school, she helped *Tante* Friede prepare the meal. Rations had reached the point where they could only manage one meal a day, but *Tante* Friede could season water and somehow make it taste good. Even if they only had a plate of lettuce, *Tante* insisted Anita make it as pretty as possible.

Mutti worked all day in a factory. They called it forced labor since, instead of pay, they were now forced to earn their tiny welfare check. The whole world had turned upside down for the Jews. The Nazis prohibited them from following their professions, took over their businesses, forbade other businesses from hiring them, forced them out of their homes, and put them on welfare. Then, when they had nothing left, the Nazis expressed outrage about them being a drain on Germany. The answer? Put them into forced labor.

If Anita thought too much about it, she wanted to scream. But, as Mutti would have patiently reminded her, screaming was dangerous. Anita remembered standing in the kitchen with Hella in their Zimpel home all those years ago and stomping her foot at something, saying, "It's not fair." Living in Nazi Germany had shredded her childlike sense of fairness.

One evening in the spring of 1941, Mutti had just taken off her coat and hat when they heard a loud knock at the door. "Open up."

Mutti grabbed Anita, her eyes widening. The knock of the *Gestapo* had finally come.

8
A Time to Mourn

Open up!" the voice repeated in harsh German. Two thundering knocks against the old wood followed. *Tante* Friede sat down suddenly as if her legs would no longer hold her. *Tante* Käte and *Tante* Elsbeth grabbed one another. Which one of them would it be?

Mutti went to the door and opened it.

"Käte Suessman?"

Tante Käte stepped forward as the color drained from her face.

"You are under arrest. Gather your things. You are allowed one bag."

No one spoke a word. Mutti went and helped her sister gather the few things to take with her.

Anita stood frozen. *Not Käte. Not now.* She looked at Käte's shaking hands running over bits and pieces of her life. What did one take to represent one's whole existence?

Mutti turned to the *Gestapo's* men. "Why do you arrest her? What crime has she committed?"

Anita's heart thudded in her chest. *No, Mutti!* Her name was already on the *blacklist. Be careful, dear Mutti. Look down. Don't draw attention to yourself.* But when she looked at *Tante* Käte's face, she watched her aunt's jaw tighten with resolve. Mutti's bravery in questioning the *SS* guard had stiffened *Tante* Käte for the ordeal ahead.

"Being a Jew is crime enough," the guard said. "Besides, I don't question things. I get my orders and make my arrests."

Tante Friede's head fell to the table as she wept. *Tante* Elsbeth crouched beside her. "You must be strong for Käte," she whispered.

"Hurry up." The younger guard watched the window. "They're already loading the others into the wagon."

Tante Käte embraced Anita, running the back of her fingers down her niece's cheek, wiping away the tears. She kneeled and kissed Friede and then slowly pulled herself up to say good-bye to Elsbeth and Mutti. She took a deep breath as if to inhale the fragrance of her family for one last time, and picked up her bag.

"Hurry up." As she stepped into the hall, one of the guards gave her a shove, causing her to stumble.

No one said a word inside the tiny room. All four watched from the window as *Tante* Käte was hurried into the wagon behind the remaining members of the Ephraim family. For once *Tante* Elsbeth did not say, "It could be worse . . ."

In the days that followed, the knocks on doors in their ghetto seemed to happen more and more frequently. To Anita it was obvious that movement of Jews out of the ghetto and into concentration camps had escalated.

Twice more knocks came to the Dittman door—first for *Tante* Friede, and then for *Tante* Elsbeth. Anita knew she'd never forget those scenes—*Tante* Friede, bent over with arthritis, clutching her small satchel of belongings, shoved into the *Gestapo* wagon; and then *Tante* Elsbeth—pale and silent.

If they had planned to take all three elderly sisters, Anita wondered why they couldn't have allowed them to stay together. The whole process was inhuman, but sometimes the intentional cruelty still surprised Anita.

Mutti thought Anita would be spared because of Vati, but Anita believed it wouldn't matter in the end. She worried it would only be a matter of time for both of them. The ghetto and even their own building became less and less crowded. In fact, as Anita walked to school she noticed many old *brownstones* completely emptied of occupants.

Amid the war, the bombing, and the heart wrenching loss, life went on. Anita went to school, did homework, and helped her mother. She felt as if she were living one of those eerie nightmares when the dreamer alternates between routine things like school and dinner to bizarre nightmarish scenes of danger and death.

In the spring of 1942, Anita completed confirmation classes with Pastor Hornig. For her confirmation Mutti managed to scrape together enough money to buy a white dress. Anita couldn't remember the last time she had a new dress. As she stood reciting all she'd learned before her much-loved congregation at St. Barbara's, the fifteen-year-old Anita felt a swelling in her spirit. She wanted to say, "Don't look at me; look to my Father."

Just a few days later, when Anita sat in class working on calculus problems, the teacher came to the side of her desk and slammed the cover of Anita's book. "Gather your things and go to the office."

She had done well in school for the year and a half she'd attended. Using Mutti's old rules of head-down, no-eye-contact, don't-draw-attention, she had somehow managed to stay out of trouble. Of course, trouble tended to come looking for Jews, so she wondered if something was wrong.

"Dittman?" The principal looked up from his desk with a question.

"*Ja*, Anita Dittman." She stood, waiting for him to invite her to take a seat.

"Here. This came from the *Gestapo*." The principal shoved a letter across the desk with a swagger of his head and shoulders. "It's high time Hitler cleansed the school of riff-raff." He waved his hand in a dismissive gesture.

What is he saying? Anita read the note. "Only Aryans may now attend school. Because of your non-Aryan status, your enrollment at König Wilhelm Gymnasium terminates immediately."

"You are dismissed, *Judenfratz*. Why do you stand in my office?"

❦ ❦ ❦ ❦

Now that Anita no longer woke early to go to school, the days seemed to run into each other. The ghetto had been emptied of all her friends. Her Christian friends could not risk being seen with her. Whenever she could borrow a book, she read. Mutti managed to keep some bits of paper and pencils from *Tante* Käte, so she continued to draw. Most of her days just seemed to slip away while she looked out the window.

Mutti worked the third shift at the Franz Becker canning plant, making jams and jellies. The heavy lifting required far more strength than a malnourished woman should have been able to muster. She went to work late at night and came home in the morning, so she needed to sleep during the day. With no way of refrigerating food, both Anita and Mutti had to stand in line every evening to get their daily rations. It took about an hour.

"God is good," Mutti said one night while they walked through the almost empty ghetto to get their rations.

"I know He is, but what makes you say that now? Your sisters are gone, our friends have been taken, the food rations have just been cut in half to all Jews, you work ten hours a day—"

"Enough already," Mutti said, poking Anita in the arm. "If you keep this up, you'll have me depressed."

Anita laughed. She couldn't help herself. This conversation was absurd. "You mean you forgot how bad things are?"

"No, *Mein Liebling.* I remembered what *Tante* Elsbeth used to say, 'It could be worse . . .'"

Anita nodded her head. How she missed her eccentric collection of aunts. "I could do with a little of Elsbeth's wisdom right now."

"Let's try to keep our spirits up, then, by thinking of why God is so good. I'll start. It could be worse than to be walking along on a beautiful fall night with one precious daughter while the other is safe in England. Thank You, Lord."

"OK, my turn. It could be worse than to be going to get food to fill an empty belly. Thank You, Lord." Anita laughed. "Can you believe I used the word *fill?* It's been a long time since I had my fill of anything."

When they got home, a letter from the *Gestapo* lay on the floor where it had been slid under the door. Neither one spoke, knowing it might very well be a summons to appear for arrest. They set about preparing supper as if nothing happened, but the letter sat on the table, dominating the whole room.

"Are we going to sit here all night looking at this awful envelope?" Anita could stand it no longer.

"No. You are right. We either trust God or we don't. No matter what the outcome, we know He keeps us in the shadow of His hand." Mutti opened the letter and read.

Anita watched her mother's face for any reaction. "What?"

Mutti let her breath out slowly. "It could be worse than for you to have to report for slave labor." She smiled. "They assigned you to Franz Becker—my factory. Had they realized, they never would have allowed it."

Anita sat down. "God is good! Oh Mutti . . ." She buried her head in her hands and let hot tears spill out.

⁕   ⁕   ⁕   ⁕

Working ten hours a day was far easier than moping alone at home. And working at the canning factory had its benefits. When the factory made apple butter, they tossed the occasional wormy apple aside. The workers were not supposed to take these, but rather than see them end up in the dustbin, Anita slipped more than one of these into her pockets. When she smuggled them home, the wormy parts could be cut out and the good bits eaten.

As they moved into winter, work extended into Sundays, so Mutti and Anita could no longer go to church. Pastor Hornig often came into the ghetto at night to bring them Communion. On Christmas of that year, Mutti and Anita found themselves with a day to attend St. Barbara's. It felt like coming home.

Pastor Hornig preached boldly, despite knowing that Nazi spies watched his every move. "God is greater than the combined evil of the entire Third *Reich*," he preached in that rich, resonant voice.

Anita believed Pastor Hornig even though Hitler's evil terrified her.

"God is in control of the war, and He's in control of your lives," he assured them. "He will preserve some of His saints."

Anita remembered the verse from Isaiah that told of the preservation of the Jewish people, "I have put my words in your mouth and covered you with the shadow of my hand—I who set the heavens in place, who laid the foundations of the earth, and who say to Zion, 'You are my people.'" *Heavenly Father, put Your words in my mouth.*

After church, Pastor Hornig took Mutti's hands in his and said, "You heard what I said about God preserving some of His true saints?"

Mutti nodded.

"I feel certain God will preserve you and Anita. You must be His witnesses no matter where He takes you."

Anita knew she would never forget that Christmas. She made a commitment to be a faithful witness, no matter what.

Anita knew they lived on borrowed time, but another year went by and they still lived quietly in the ghetto. Anita had been moved to a wine-bottling factory, but the pattern of work, food lines, and sleep continued.

She and Mutti found new hope that winter as the Nuremberg law passed. It stated that if a Jewish man or woman had ever been married to a German, they were protected from arrest or concentration camps as long as they did not revert to the Jewish faith. All children born to those marriages were protected as well.

Pastor Hornig warned Mutti not to put too much stock in the law. He'd already seen it violated more than once. But Mutti felt it represented one more protection.

So when an early dawn knock came on a cold January day, Mutti was not prepared.

"Quick, Anita, look out the window. That cannot be the *Gestapo*, neh?"

Anita's stomach twisted as she saw the *Gestapo* wagon with *SS* guards fanning out in several directions. She recognized the drill and looked at Mutti. No words passed between them.

Mutti leaned her head against the door for just a moment.

Anita recognized the posture of resignation. As she opened the door, the *SS* guards only saw strength.

"Hilde Dittman? You have three minutes to pack one small bag. You are being arrested." The older officer barked these orders like he could say them in his sleep. Mutti had to sign a paper stating that everything in the apartment belonged to her. A younger guard took red labels and tagged all the furniture.

Except for the throbbing ache in her stomach and the swelling of her throat, Anita felt numb.

"Your possessions now belong to the state. A careful inventory of your things will be taken and someone will be by later to pick them all up." He stood first on one foot and then the other as if irritated that the efficient process required explanation.

"What about the Nuremberg laws?" Mutti's voice held the edge of desperation. "I married a German and I'm a Christian."

The *SS* guard laughed a loud explosive laugh. "What are you, lady? A lawyer?" He continued to laugh as if that was the funniest thing he'd heard.

"You cannot tag all the furniture. It belongs to my daughter." Mutti sounded outraged.

"We didn't tag her bed. If she wants the rest, the *Gestapo* will sell it back to her." His impatience boiled over. "Step it up, Hans, get on with it. Dittman's got pitiful few things as it is."

With that, the younger man finished tagging and logging the last piece. He turned to Anita. "You can ride along with us to the *synagogue* where we will hold the prisoners if you like and say good-bye to your mother there."

"Thank you. I will." It would give Anita and Mutti a little longer.

"I need to use the bathroom, young man." Mutti said to him, in that motherlike voice of hers that allowed no argument.

He shrugged an approval of sorts while the other man began looking antsy.

Mutti went inside. When she came out, she nodded her daughter toward the bathroom. Anita understood that Mutti must've left a message.

"Please wait while I go." Anita stepped inside before anything could be said. There on the edge of the sink lay a tiny leather purse containing a modest bundle of money. It represented every penny Mutti had been able to save. Anita tucked it into her waistband and came out.

"All right. Let's go," said the older man.

As he loaded them into the wagon, he raised his eyebrow at Anita as if to say, "This won't be the last time you make a trip in a *Gestapo* wagon."

9
Summoned by Name

When the *Gestapo* guard forced Anita to leave the old *synagogue* where Mutti had been taken, the mother and daughter only had enough time to embrace. Words were far less important than the familiar physical closeness. Anita breathed deeply to take in the very scent of Mutti—that mixture of soap, lavender, and sugary-fruity scent of the jam factory. How she would miss Mutti.

As she followed the guard out, Anita turned for one last look. "Until the Lord reunites us again, Mutti . . ." She lifted her hand to her mouth and blew a pretend kiss across the yard.

Mutti smiled.

Earlier, Mutti had made Anita write down her father's telephone number. "Call him to see if he can help you buy back some of the furniture."

Anita didn't feel like calling him. Her stomach burned. She also knew she couldn't bear to go home to the lonely room filled with red-tagged furniture. She walked toward St. Barbara's and Pastor Hornig.

"How we will miss your mother," Pastor Hornig said when Anita poured out her story. "I still feel as strongly as I ever did that God will protect her."

Anita needed to hear those words.

"When will she leave and where will she go?" the pastor asked.

"I don't think she leaves until tomorrow. I'm not sure, but I think she'll go to Theresienstadt in Czechoslovakia." It sounded so far away to Anita.

"That's good news, Anita. Very good news, because they still allow mail and packages at Theresienstadt." Pastor Hornig seemed to be thinking. "Perhaps you can visit her tonight to take food. I'll ask Frau Hornig to prepare some sandwiches and a little fruit."

As he left to arrange the food, Anita realized she felt better. Pastor Hornig was right—if she could write to Mutti, it would keep her mother's spirits up and Anita wouldn't be as lonely. *Dear Heavenly Father, make it possible for me to send something to Mutti each week. Keep us close. Bring us back to each other at the end . . .*

"Here." Pastor Hornig handed her a small package. "Do your best to get in to see her tonight. Tell her we will pray her through this. Remind her that she rests in the shadow of the Almighty hand."

When Anita arrived at the makeshift prison, she saw Steffi

Bott, the daughter of one of her mother's friends, along with the three Wolf brothers—Gerhard, Wolfgang, and Rudi.

"Was your mother taken?" Steffi asked after greeting Anita.

"Yes. How did you know?"

"My mother's in there, too, along with Frau Wolf. Seems like the Nazis went after Jewish Christians in this sweep."

"All three of our mothers were married to Germans," Rudi said. "So much for the new Nuremberg laws."

"Are you here for a last visit?" Anita asked.

"We tried," Steffi said. "They won't let us in."

"They must! I have food and her favorite old pink chenille bathrobe." That sounded silly in the face of a concentration camp, but Anita knew it would comfort Mutti. "I didn't get to properly say good-bye." Anita thought of so many things she forgot to say.

"Shhh. Gerhard figured a way in, through that old hotel over there," Rudi said. "It used to be part of the *synagogue* that now houses the prisoners. All we have to do is slip by the desk clerk. Besides, who'd ever expect someone to try to sneak *into* a prison?"

While Rudi and Wolfgang distracted the clerk, the other three slipped down the stairs leading to the basement. The way in was complicated—through a basement, down through an underground tunnel. At the end of the tunnel, they could see a door, slightly ajar, leading into the basement of the *synagogue*. Prisoners milled around inside the basement, but right in front of the door stood the *Gestapo* guard. None of their mothers seemed to be in the room. The three waited for a long time until the guard stepped out of the room.

Gerhard pushed the door open. A woman looked at him, her eyes growing large with fear. "Leave at once. You will get us in trouble."

"We want to see our mothers—Frau Dittman, Frau Bott, and Frau Wolf. We have these packages for them." He pushed the packages into the room. "If we get caught, can you see that they get these?"

"*Ja, ja.* Now go."

At that moment, they heard the clomp of heavy footsteps in the tunnel. Gerhard pulled the door shut.

"What are you doing?" The guard practically yelled in Anita's face.

None of the three said a word. Anita's stomach twisted into a knot of fear.

"Come. You will join your friends in the *Gestapo* office."

After what seemed like the longest time—a time that included many questions and whispered conferences between guards—the five stood before the *Gestapo*. "You committed a crime punishable by death. You know that, don't you?"

Steffi kept her head down. Her tears dripped onto the floor. Anita prayed silently and knew that her friends did the same.

"I do not have time for the likes of you today," the *Gestapo* said. "I shall have to release you—although it's against my best judgment. Do not think you escaped easily." He opened a big book. "I'm recording each of your names on the *blacklist*. We shall deal with you at a later date."

As they left to go to their homes, they thanked God over and over. "If we had not been released," Anita said, "we'd never be able to keep food packages going to our mothers."

"Being *blacklisted* hardly worries me," Rudi said. "Even with the Nuremberg laws, it's only a matter of time until we are summoned."

Though they'd known of each other through their mothers, after their close call at the *synagogue*, the five became friends.

"Vati?" Anita had gone to Pastor Hornig's to place the long distance telephone call to her father who'd moved sixty miles away in Sorau.

"Anita?" The voice on the other end of the scratchy telephone line sounded surprised. "What is wrong?"

"Mutti's been taken. She's on her way to Theresienstadt."

"Oh, no, not Hilde. I thought she'd be safe." Distress colored his words.

Vati's reaction encouraged Anita. "Mutti told me to call you if I ever needed help."

"What can I do?"

"They've taken all our furniture and possessions except my bed. I can buy back some furniture and a few of my personal things, but the *Gestapo* inflated the price way above anything I can afford." Anita didn't wait for him to answer. She didn't know if she could handle yet another rejection. "They want one thousand *marks*."

"I'll get you the money tomorrow, daughter—" He sounded like he wanted to say more. "I'm so glad you asked."

When Anita hung up the phone, she needed a moment to compose herself. She knew her relationship with Vati would never be whole, but today was the first time they had connected.

"Wouldn't Hilde be pleased to hear of this?" Pastor Hornig said after Anita recounted the conversation. "You know God will not allow us to harbor bitterness, no matter how much right we have to it. You've taken a hard step today, young friend. God will honor you for it."

"But I called asking him a favor."

"When we are at odds, sometimes the easiest way to reach out is to allow the person to do something for us." Pastor Hornig smiled. "And sometimes that's the hardest thing to do. It's much easier for us to keep our backs stiff and hang on to our pride." He sat back in his chair. "You allowed your father to come into your life in a way that made him feel invited. Remember your telling me about the fancy toys your father used to like to buy?"

"Ja."

"Your father may not be able to speak words of love. He is clumsy with emotions and words. He feels most comfortable giving gifts. You let him give the only kind of love he knows how to offer."

Pastor Hornig always gave Anita something to think about.

Anita remembered all those years ago when Hella remarked about how easy it was to fall into a routine, no matter how much the situation around you unraveled. Anita fell into just such a routine—working hard and saving every penny she could scrape together. Each week she used her ration card to buy Mutti a loaf of fresh dark pumpernickel bread. The bread was perfect, because it was so dense, it shipped well and lasted almost indefinitely.

Mutti sent postcards back to Anita, thanking her for the bread. Anita knew it was more than bread—those loaves became a link from mother to daughter.

Because Anita sent the weekly bread along with anything else she managed to tuck into the food package, she tried to get by with next to nothing to save her ration card for Mutti's food. She expected to drop weight and lose hair like she did when she starved in Berlin. This time she never lost an ounce of weight and had all the energy she'd ever need. What a mystery. She couldn't explain it. She just kept repeating Mutti's words, "God is good." If nothing else, having to rely on God for everything allowed Anita to see her Father's protection.

One week, as she went to the bakery to buy her usual loaf of pumpernickel, Anita couldn't shake the feeling she ought to buy hard, dry zwieback bread instead. It didn't make sense. Mutti loved pumpernickel, and the heavy flour and rich molasses filled it with nutrition. Would mother be disappointed if she received crusty zwieback instead? Anita gave in to that nagging feeling and bought the zwieback.

Several weeks later, Mutti wrote to tell of being desperately sick and unable to hold any food down. She told how dangerous it was to be sick in camp. The guards often considered sickness a problem, and they liked to make their problems disappear. She didn't say anything more than those cryptic words, but Anita knew what she meant.

Mutti wrote that she remembered back to Zimpel days. Whenever one of them couldn't keep food down, zwieback always did the trick. The more she thought about it, the more she longed for dry zwieback to help settle her stomach. That same day Anita's package arrived—filled with the very zwieback Mutti craved.

That zwieback strengthened both Mutti's and Anita's faith. God listened to Mutti's needs and managed to communicate them to Anita. As Mutti wrote to Anita, "Is there any doubt that the Lord will continue to provide for both of us?"

They needed that kind of reassurance. Even though the German people did not fully know about the death camps, the Jewish people did. Hitler did his best to keep it secret, but a few Jews returned. With the accounts from those eye-witnesses and the coded messages smuggled out, Anita knew the likely future for Mutti and eventually for herself as well.

Theresienstadt had been built as a "model" ghetto—it was actually an old walled city, now filled with Jews. Once in a while, Hitler's men would spiff things up and give a group of dignitaries a tour of a few select places in an effort to show them that the rumors were not true. In fact, Theresienstadt was a vermin-infested, overcrowded camp used as a temporary stopover. Every day the guards loaded prisoners onto transport vehicles taking them to the dreaded Auschwitz. Just as Mutti suspected, all those years ago, Hitler's final solution—after gathering the Jews into smaller and tighter knots of concentration—was to make them disappear entirely.

Anita prayed that Mutti would be kept safe until Hitler was stopped.

By Anita's seventeenth birthday, Hitler no longer seemed invincible. The Allies—those armies fighting against Germany—began to score victories. The bombing grew more intense; but Anita understood that, even though the bombs were frightening, Hitler must be defeated. Every day she prayed for her three aunts, for friends from the ghetto, for Frau Bott, Frau Wolf, and all the others. Mostly she prayed for Mutti.

But for some reason, the knock had not yet come to her door. She passed another summer in the now almost-empty ghetto by spending free time with Rudi, Wolfgang, Gerhard, and Steffi. St. Barbara's continued to be her family. And there were always hours and hours spent in the office at the factory.

"Anita." Her boss came into the front office where she had just finished filing the orders that had been filled that August day. "There's someone on the telephone who wishes to speak to you." He stood and watched her. No one had ever called her on the telephone. Her hand shook as she picked up the receiver.

"Anita?" It was Steffi.

"What's wrong?"

Steffi burst into tears. "I received a summons to appear at the train station tomorrow at ten in the morning."

"A summons?" Anita was confused. *No knock? No guards?*

"Maybe because we are Christian and half Aryan? I don't know . . ." Steffi hardly made sense. "Because you are *blacklisted* with me, I wanted to give you warning that you may get a summons as well."

Anita looked over at the boss who hadn't moved. "If so, we'll go together."

Steffi continued to cry on the other end of the phone. Anita thought about what Pastor Hornig had said about being a bold witness. *Stand there if you like, Herr Boss, I shall speak the truth to my friend.* "Steffi, don't cry. God will protect us. He will shadow us with His very hand."

Steffi coughed and then said, "Thank you. How I need reminding sometimes."

"I need to get back to work. *Auf Wiedersehen,* Steffi."

When Anita got home after work, a summons awaited her as well. At least she and Steffi would be together. As she let the letter fall from her hands, she prayed. The words that came to mind were the ones she remembered the priest say on that day all those years ago when she met Jesus in the stained glass windows: "I will never leave you nor forsake you."

10

Sets the Prisoners Free

Anita read the letter carefully and followed the instructions. One bag would be allowed, so she took her knapsack and carefully packed one change of clothing, a small pan, a bowl, a cake of soap, and eating utensils. Though the instructions warned against bringing anything else, Anita wrapped her Bible in a clean cloth and put it deep into her knapsack.

She couldn't stop thinking about Mutti. Would she worry when the letters and packages stopped? News of arrests, travel, and guard movement were considered war secrets, so she could not write openly to either Mutti or Pastor Hornig. *At least I can send bread one last time.* Anita ran, hoping to get to the bakery before closing to get one more loaf of bread to send to Theresienstadt for Mutti. She arrived just in time to pick out a freshly wrapped two-pound loaf. As she walked home, she got an idea.

She would try to smuggle a note to Mutti inside the loaf of

bread so that when the food and letters stopped, her mother would know. It was risky. Mutti hinted in her letters that the guards sometimes stole the food meant for prisoners. If a guard should find the note, it could be dangerous for Mutti. Was it worth the risk? *Heavenly Father, protect this bread. Protect Mutti.*

Anita took a tiny piece of paper and wrote the following words: "Dear Mutti, I am going to a camp tomorrow so I won't be able to send any more food for a while. Don't worry about me. I will be all right. We will soon be united. Love, Anita."

The loaf was wrapped in the usual cellophane with a label at the end. Anita carefully peeled back the label. Taking a long thin knife she cut a slot into the loaf and tucked her note deep inside. She pressed the label back onto the cellophane. The loaf looked perfect. She trusted God to work out the rest.

If only she could get word to Pastor Hornig—but she knew her pastor and the family at St. Barbara's would pray every day for her just as they already prayed for Mutti and so many others.

When she got to the train station the next morning, Steffi ran over and grabbed Anita's hands. "I'm so frightened, but I'm so glad we will be together. Where do you think they will take us?"

"I don't know, but this is different from the way our mothers were taken." Anita squeezed her friend's hand. "It's not just the two of us; God goes with us as well."

"In fact, it's not just the five of us!" Rudi Wolf had come up behind her. All three of the Wolf brothers had received summons as well.

"Look around," Gerhard said. "There are twenty of us from St. Barbara's alone."

"This must have been a last sweep. Look at how many of us are Christian Jews or have one Aryan parent," Rudi said.

"Who said you could talk?" One of the *SS* men screamed at them and used his stick to give Rudi a shove. "Get on board, you lousy *Juden*."

Steffi started to cry, but Anita hurried her on the train. Just when they thought their car was as full as it could possibly be, more people would be pushed on.

"At least these are trains with windows and seats," Anita said to Steffi who sat between Anita and the window. "These are not the usual boxcars or cattle cars."

Steffi didn't answer.

"Anita." Rudi, who was seated with his brothers in the seat behind them, leaned over the seat. "If I heard right, we're being taken to—"

Two *SS* men walked down the crowded aisle of the car, guns drawn. When they passed, Rudi continued, "Barthold. It's a work camp near Schmiegrode."

"Halt den Mund!" The SS guard hit the edge of Rudi's seat with the butt of his gun as he told them to shut up. "You may not talk unless instructed to do so."

The train rattled over the countryside with little more than groans and sounds of weeping. Anita could see the reflection of Steffi in the sooty window. She looked stricken. *Dear God, be with my fellow passengers. Be with me. Help us to face uncertainty knowing You go ahead of us.* She opened her knapsack, dug deep inside, and showed Steffi the corner of her Bible. For the first time, Steffi smiled ever so slightly.

After about two hours, the train clanged to a halt amid belching smoke and screeching breaks. "Get off. Get off." The *SS* men jumped out first and began barking orders. When some didn't move fast enough, a hobnail boot sent them sprawling.

The women gathered on one side, the men on the other, and each group set off—prodded by guards—in a different direction. Anita counted about 150 women. As they walked through the town, she wondered what the residents thought. When they left town, they walked into the woods for about a mile until they came to an old farm.

"That," the guard pointed to the old milking barn, "will be your quarters."

The looks on the women's faces told the story. *This many women in one milking barn?*

"Men will be housed over in the horse barn." He pointed across the meadow. Relief showed on the faces of those who had come with husbands, brothers, or sons. When the guards had separated the two groups, who knew if they'd ever see one another again?

"You must thank *der Führer* for his kindness." The guard stopped, but got a stony response. "You will work, but you will be paid—perhaps the only prisoners in the country to be paid—twenty *marks* a month."

Several women raised eyebrows ever so slightly as if to say they'd believe it when they saw the money in their hands.

He picked up an enameled basin. "You can wash in a basin or out in the creek over there. Toilets are out back. They are open-ditch toilets, but you'll get used to them." He laughed. "You may not get used to the guards who like to hang out near there, but if you have to go badly enough . . ."

Steffi shivered beside Anita in spite of the hot August day. Anita hoped her friend could toughen up enough to stand this. Steffi's parents had sheltered her much more than Anita had been sheltered.

"Like all of Germany right now, you'll work a ten-hour day. If it rains, you'll get a day off." He laughed. "Unfortunately, it hasn't rained all summer long."

"As soon as the cooks get set up, you'll have dinner—a bowl of soup. They'll also give you a slice of bread, but save that for your morning rations. You'll have nothing more until your soup at noon." With that the guard showed them into their quarters and spent most of the afternoon giving rules and more rules—few of which Anita could remember.

As she made her way through the long line that night to get a ladleful of soup splashed in her bowl, she realized these would be hungry times. The grayish soup looked like dirty dishwater with wood shavings in it. It didn't taste much better. She took the slice of bread and wrapped it in a hankie and laid it beside her pillow. Her stomach growled so fiercely, she longed to eat it, but she knew she'd need the strength to do a day's work.

In the morning, only a few crumbs remained amid the rodent droppings—rats had eaten her entire morning rations. Anita started work on an empty stomach. They dug ditches from morning until night in the hot August sun. The trenches were over six feet deep, built to stop Russian tanks from crossing into Nazi territory. Anita, at barely five feet tall, had all she could do to scramble out of the ditch at night.

"How will we work like this on so little food?" Steffi's hands were blistered and her face sunburned.

"I don't know. The only way we can do it will be with God's help." Anita prided herself on being strong and athletic, but every muscle in her body ached. "I keep hearing that the Allies are advancing and Hitler will be toppled. Let's pray that's true."

The work did go on and, if anything, the rations got lighter. Month after month, they all lost weight. The only bright spot in the camp was Anita's Bible study held in the corner of the cow barn nearly every night. Some of the woman came once but did not stay; others who'd been strong Christians in Breslau became angry with God. Those who studied found their faith blossomed despite the work camp.

Sometimes Anita worked alongside the men. They were not supposed to talk, but some guards were less strict than others.

"I hear from some of the sympathetic farmers in the area that Germany falters in the war," Rudi spoke in the lowest whisper.

"Be careful. Any talk of the war progress is strictly *verboten*." Anita had seen a man beaten and stomped for this.

"I'm careful, but I keep my ear to the ground." Rudi smiled. "There's reason to hope."

Anita kept on hoping, but things at camp grew worse. The lice became so bad the women could hardly work. They wanted to tear the scalp off their heads. The guards finally managed to get some medicine for the lice. It seemed to work, but it burned their skin and everyone lost great patches of hair.

Anita was glad Barthold had no mirrors. Her skin had tanned to a leathery brown from working day after day in the hot sun. She'd lost so much weight that every bone on her back stuck out; and now that she was half-bald from malnutrition and lice medicine, the picture must be complete. *Don't let me be ungrateful, Lord. I live and I still hope to find Mutti after the war. Let me continue to be Your witness.*

Several months into her stay, the guards announced that prisoners could use the telephone to call someone from their family. They could invite that person to visit at the camp next Sunday. For the first time since they arrived, hope and excitement infused the workers.

Anita had no one to call but Vati. *Would he even want to come?* "Hello, Vati?" she said into the camp phone.

"Anita? Is that you?" His voice sounded shaky. "They told me you were taken. Are you well?"

"I'm at Barthold, near Schmiegrode. They gave us permission to invite family to visit next Sunday." Anita couldn't bring herself to ask.

"May I come, Anita?"

Her tears kept her from answering right away, but she managed to say, "Please."

People were lined up to use the phone, so Anita managed to say good-bye. *He wants to come.* She could hardly believe it.

Vati came early that Sunday. Anita could see him waiting until the guards let him come into camp. He kept scanning all the women, trying to find her. She dared not raise her arm, but she willed him to find her. *Look at me, Vati. Look at me.* Finally their eyes met. She saw a brief look of horror pass over his face before he schooled his features. *I guess I won't win any beauty contests.*

When he finally joined her, he embraced her and held her gently for the longest time. Anita couldn't remember Vati's embrace. Had he ever hugged her before? He seemed uncomfortable when he realized how emotional he was.

"I brought you food." He held out his knapsack.

"Come; let's sit over here on the meadow." She saw how happy he was to have brought food. It made her think about what Pastor Hornig had said about Vati showing love through giving.

They visited until the guard announced it was time for the visitors to leave.

"I'll come back if they let me," Vati said in a gravelly voice.

They embraced once more before Vati left to walk back to the train. Anita watched him walk away until she could see him no longer.

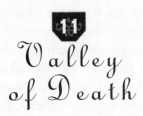

11
Valley
of Death

"Do you hear those sounds?" Rudi crept up behind her as she put away her tools for the day.

"The thunder?" She listened. "I've never been afraid of thunder."

"That's not thunder." He stopped while another thunder-clap seemed to shake the earth. "Russian *migs*."

"How do you know?" Rudi amazed Anita. He seemed to know everything.

"The German farmers around here are sympathetic to our plight. I made friends with one. Luckily, he has a *wireless*." Rudi winked at her before slipping away.

Anita sensed a change in the guards. They were tense and more watchful, but trainloads of prisoners continued to arrive each week. By November, Anita guessed that camp population swelled past five hundred.

"Pack up your belongings," the guard said through a bullhorn. "We're moving camp. There's no time to waste."

With almost no notice, they left Camp Barthold after more than three months there. It hardly mattered. The new camp near Ostlinde was much the same as the old camp—a little more crowded perhaps. They still worked ten-hour days, starting at five in the morning, but now they cut and stacked trees from the forest as a second line of defense behind the trenches they had built back at Barthold.

Time continued to pass slowly, much as it did in Barthold—with work, very little sleep, and very little food. The one bright spot was Bible study. The deeper into winter it got, the colder it became. Anita couldn't remember a month so cold as that January in 1945.

"I've got news," Rudi came up behind her in the forest.

"You're going to get us in trouble yet." Anita loved to hear the news, but she knew the penalty.

"How can we keep up our spirits if we don't share good news?" Rudi's eyes still twinkled. "The Russians advance on the *Reich* at this very moment." He raised his axe and brought it down with a resounding crack.

Anita could see that a guard came near, but she'd already heard all she needed to hear. *Keep Mutti safe until the Russians or the Allies liberate Theresienstadt. And let me make it back to her.*

The next time Anita and Steffi worked near Rudi, he managed to slip bits of information to them between guard rounds. "Bad news, according to the farmer near us. Some concentration camps have been liberated already, but what they are finding—"

The girls worked along in silence for a time, waiting until it was safe for Rudi to talk again.

"—Hitler mounted a massive extermination of the Jews in these last days. Six hundred thousand killed at Auschwitz alone in the weeks since we've been here—"

As they heard the crunch of a hobnail boot on the frosty forest floor, Steffi and Anita began to sing an old German folksong. Singing was one of the few things allowed. The guards thought it made the workers go faster. They kept singing, even when Rudi whispered to them. It covered his words.

"The Russians may be at Theresienstadt . . . not sure. But things are much worse there than we thought." He swung his axe high into the air and brought it down in a smooth arc.

"Typhoid. My new friend heard on his *wireless* that Theresienstadt is now considered one of the worst camps— like Auschwitz and Treblinka." He swung his axe for a while again until it was safe. "We need to keep praying for our mothers. . . . Miracle—we need a miracle."

Anita did pray.

One night that January the guards called a formation at nine-thirty. The weather blustered and threatened snow, and the ragtag bunch of prisoners felt the wind cutting right through their thin clothing.

"Pack your things. Immediately. We leave on foot in five minutes." The guard seemed as confused as the prisoners.

Again? Hadn't they just moved from Barthold a couple

months ago? They were trying to outrun the Russians. Anita could sense it.

She saw Rudi smile from across the formation. In that moment, she knew that he and his brothers would use the confusion to slip away and escape. She silently sent him a good-bye. *Be with my friends, Lord. Whatever they face, give them strength.* He winked and then was gone. How did three nearly-six-feet-tall boys manage to slip away so quietly?

She and Steffi didn't have time to think about it. They packed as quickly as they could and joined the long queue of women preparing for the hike. Anita looked down at her worn wooden shoes. How she wished she had boots for this wintertime trek.

"Anita, I'm not sure I can do this." Steffi's voice faltered.

Anita didn't know how to answer. She'd worked all day too. Could they make it? She honestly didn't know. "Look up at those shadows across the moon, Steffi. Doesn't it remind you of Pastor Hornig's verse about God covering us with the shadow of His hand?" The cold air made Anita's teeth chatter. "Let's do the best we can and trust Him to protect us whether we can make it or not."

"I wish I had your faith, Anita," Steffi said. "I feel like running and never coming back."

"I know." Anita did know. She could hardly walk another step and the farther they went, the deeper the snow. "Just remember—no matter how bad things get, you'll never outrun God."

Anita's limping grew worse. Early on, she'd raised a blister on her heel. She dared not let on that anything was wrong. Guards preferred to shoot lame prisoners rather than deal with them. By the time they finally stopped, her whole leg was swollen and mottled.

Steffi came and crouched down by her, handing her a note. "If anything happens to me, will you give this to my mother?"

"Nothing is going to happen to you, Steffi. Stop saying things like that. You're scaring me." Anita felt close to tears.

Steffi smiled at Anita. "I didn't think anything scared you." She sat quietly for a time. "If I were to disappear, this has the address of some friends in Bavaria where Mother could find me after the war."

Anita finally understood what she meant. "If you left, I would miss you terribly, but you know I would pray for you every day until I heard you were safe." She put her arm around her friend.

"I know."

After walking for days, they finally came to their new camp in the deserted town of Grunberg. The men and women were housed in empty buildings. At this camp they were assigned busywork—each day the prisoners walked more than a mile to a huge pile of rubble. Piece by piece, they had to move the pile to one side of the road and then move it back again.

Just a few days later, Steffi was gone. No one saw her leave and nothing more was heard from her. How Anita missed her.

❧   ❧   ❧   ❧

"If I have to move this pile of rubble one more time, I may very well scream and bring all these *SS* men down on our heads!" Hella Frommelt said. She worked alongside Anita now that Steffi had disappeared. Anita had known Hella Frommelt since she had first joined Anita's Bible study at Barthold. Working together, they grew closer and closer. Anita always smiled to look at this Hella—so different from Anita's sister, Hella.

"If screaming would do any good, I'd join you. Right now, screaming would feel good since the more I'm on my leg, the more it swells." Anita lowered her voice. "At least busywork is better than helping Hitler's cause against the Allies." She stopped talking while a guard nervously hurried over to make sure they kept busy. When he left, Anita leaned in toward Hella. "If you look at the guards, you can read how the war's going on their faces." She could practically smell their fear as they rushed by.

As she reached down for another piece of stone, the ground shook and the sound of cannon fire made them all put their hands over their ears. All but a couple of guards ran toward their makeshift headquarters.

"It's got to be Russian cannons." The sound and the percussion reminded her of the Berlin bombings. Her stomach twisted at the thought. Someone had to stop Hitler, but Anita understood the cost. She pictured the devastation in Berlin. "Before this war is over, I fear that nothing will be left standing in Germany."

"Germany and Hitler must pay." Hella said quietly.

"You know the funny thing?" *As if anything were funny.* "God will call us Christians to forgive Germany." Anita put her hands over her ears as the sound of another volley seemed to ricochet off the trees. "Besides, the German people themselves have little to do with the horrors perpetrated by Hitler—I wonder how many know what's been happening? Look at these farmers here and near Barthold and Ostlinde. As soon as they saw what the *Reich* did, they did everything they could to help us."

"I know. If I live, my hardest calling will be to follow Christ in this." Hella set the charred log she'd been moving onto the pile and sat down on top of it. With the guards preoccupied, why bother pretending to work?

Anita sat next to her and propped her swollen leg onto a stone. "I don't know how many times I read the story about when Jesus forgives those who crucified Him . . . but it wasn't until recently that I began to grasp the enormity of that act." Anita sighed. "Just think; it would be like walking into one of those gassing rooms at Auschwitz and stopping to ask God to forgive Hitler and all the guards—even the very ones pushing us to our deaths."

"I think it's impossible unless you are God," Hella said.

"Or unless you have the Spirit of God inside you." The cannon and *artillery* fire seemed to grow louder. "Do you think we should take cover or something?"

"Go to the town. Return to your quarters." A guard came from the direction of their barracks and began shouting orders. "Now! Hurry!"

Another guard came carrying his rifle. He'd put a *bayonet* on the end. "March quickly."

The group of workers hurried back to the brick building that housed them in the center of Grunberg. Anita limped to keep up with them. As soon as the guards finished counting heads, they sealed the door. Anita found a spot at the window and rubbed at the grime on the glass, making a circle to see out. The guards ringed the building, *bayonets* at ready. *Were they keeping the prisoners in or trying to keep others out?* The crowded room was bathed in fear. Women sobbed openly.

Anita's leg throbbed. When the sliver of the moon cast a little light across the floor she tried to get a look at the leg—it seemed to be dark, almost black, and was hot to the touch. *All this from a blister? Lord, not now!*

The bombardment continued. If the building were hit, would they be locked inside without possibility of escape? With the stories of Russian cruelty and reports of the *atrocities* they committed, Anita and Hella wondered if they should be more afraid of their Nazi keepers or of the Russian liberators. No one slept that night as the attack intensified.

With morning light came quiet.

The guards burst into the room with *bayonets* crossed. "Gather your things."

Anita tried to rise, but pains shot up her leg. How could she march again? *Lord Jesus, You must make a way!*

As Anita limped out into the cold morning, there stood two old horse carts.

"Get on, get on!" The butt of a rifle against her back propelled her forward. Hella, who'd already climbed onto the cart, reached both arms down and took Anita's arm and pulled her up. The rough wood of the cart scraped her leg, and the pain nearly caused her one good knee to buckle.

"Don't let them see that you're hurting, Anita," Hella whispered.

As the women settled, the drivers took off. Their driver was a Polish prisoner of war, pressed into the task. The carts rolled down the dirt road. Anita felt every bump and pothole. She clenched her teeth and squeezed her eyes shut to keep from screaming in pain. *Father . . . help!*

Anita must have slept since the sun had risen in the sky. They still bumped along the road. Those women who left behind husbands or friends cried softly. Others looked numb. The only guards were two *SS* on bicycles following at a great distance, absurdly trying to pedal through the deep snow.

"Anita, are you awake?" Hella whispered. "Those guards can't possibly keep up with us. If we escaped, they'd have to stay with the carts."

"You may be right. Let's ask God to show us the perfect time." Anita looked at the deep snowdrifts all around and knew their trail could easily be followed if anyone still cared to do so. As she spoke, their destination came into view—a deserted death camp with barbed wire around the fences.

"I want to bribe the driver somehow," Anita said.

"That won't work. If he were caught, he'd pay with his life." Hella shook her head. "Besides, all I have is twenty *marks*."

At that moment three of the other girls decided to make a run for it into the woods. "Come with us," one of the girls said.

"I can't." Anita pulled her dress up and showed her leg.

"And I'm staying with Anita," Hella said.

"Do any of you have a pack of cigarettes?" Anita knew cigarettes often worked as good bribes.

"Here," said one of the women, tossing an unopened package of cigarettes at Anita before the three of them jumped off and ran into the woods.

Anita couldn't breathe for fear, but no one chased after the girls. *Thank You, Jesus.*

"Get off," shouted one of the guards as he finally caught up to the slowing cart. "Get off and file into those gates up ahead." One by one, the frightened women jumped or fell off the carts. You could see from the looks on their faces those who recognized a death camp. Anita held back. She did not want to get down in front of the guard. He'd know about her bad leg as soon as she tried to move.

When there were only a handful of women left, the guard said, "I need two of you to get supplies for the camp."

"Hella and I will go." Anita wondered if this was the chance she prayed for.

He gave them directions and gave further instructions to the driver. As the gate clanged shut behind their fellow prisoners, the cart took off down the road. Anita prayed, asking God to preserve their friends. They scooted up closer to the driver.

"Please sir, take us to the train station." Anita held out the package of cigarettes and the money.

Hella's eyes widened. Anita knew what she thought—they'd just put their lives into a stranger's hands.

"Pray," she whispered to Hella.

The driver smiled and held out his hand for the bribe. *Will he really risk his life for so paltry a bribe?*

"Do you know where the train station is located?" Anita wondered if she misinterpreted his seeming agreement.

"Ja, ja."

He clucked at the horse to trot and off they went. A short distance from the camp, the train station came into view. Anita asked him to let them off since she saw armed Nazi soldiers patrolling the station. The man tipped his hat and winked at them as they jumped down.

Anita's leg buckled as she landed. *Not now, Lord!*

They walked toward the train station. "Try to look like we are village girls, fearfully running away from the Russians." Anita figured in the confusion of people fleeing the invaders and because the death camp looked long deserted, no one would suspect work camp escapees.

Just as they stepped up onto the train platform, the three girls who'd escaped earlier came out of the woods. *Good. We'll look like separate groups of friends from the village who know each other.*

They greeted their friends, and while Hella quietly filled them in on the plan, Anita spoke to one of the soldiers. "Sir, we've been advised to flee the Russians. We've heard of their brutality, and our parents want us to seek safety out of town. They left last week, and we will join them in Sorau."

The soldier smiled at her. "Those blonde braids remind me of my little sister. It's been a long war." He shook his head. "I hope she's not in this kind of danger." He pointed to a captured Russian tank chained to a flatcar. "That's our ride. I can ask my superior if he'd mind us giving aid to five frightened German girls, but it might be crowded inside the tank."

Anita smiled. "Since the war we've lost weight. We hardly take up any room."

He laughed and went to ask permission.

"He probably thinks this will make a great story to tell after the war—inside a demolished tank, atop a flatbed car, and crammed in with five young girls." Hella laughed. "It's story enough, but if he only knew the real story."

With permission granted, the soldier helped the girls into the tank. As they got settled, they felt the jerk of the train and knew they were on their way. The clang of train wheels against the track seemed to reverberate against the metal of the tank. The chains holding the tank onto the flatbed car screeched and clunked, but inside the wrecked tank they knew they headed to freedom. After thanking God, Anita let the rhythmic clanking rock her to sleep as the soldier listened to his *wireless*.

When she awoke, she could see through the shredded metal that it was dark. The other girls stirred as well. Their flight from Grünberg had left them exhausted. "Where are we?" Anita awakened fully. "Did we miss Sorau?"

"*Ja*. Sadly, the Russians are massing to overtake Sorau. I decided to let you sleep and wake you when we get to Berlin."

Anita knew they dared not go to Berlin. Hella had German relatives in Bautzen. "Can you let us out when we stop at Fürstenwalde? We'll get a train for Dresden and change to Bautzen."

"I can do that, but you know that train service is unreliable with the war." He seemed sad to say good-bye.

When the train stopped at Fürstenwalde, Anita said "I pray you see your little sister soon." He lifted them out of the tank. "Thank you."

As she stepped onto the platform, shards of pain streaked up her leg. Her thigh was nearly double its normal size. As she looked down at it, she realized that the Lord not only allowed her to escape, but she hadn't had to walk more than a couple of steps. Her leg needed care, but she knew He had spared her. He must have a reason for the leg as well.

"We leave you here," the three friends said. "Our people

are in Rostock." They were some of the few in camp who'd actually received a tiny portion of their promised wages. They had just about enough to purchase tickets and catch the waiting train.

"I gave you all my money for that bribe," Hella said. "Do you have any good ideas?"

Anita reached deep into the now-ragged knapsack and pulled out the purse Mutti left for her all those months ago. "I've saved this money to one day try to buy my mother's freedom as some were able to do, but rumors are that Theresienstadt has already been liberated." She clenched the purse. "More than anything I need to get to my mother."

They took some of the money and bought their tickets to Bautzen, with a change of trains in Dresden.

Less than an hour later they sat side by side in seats on a train—like normal German citizens—looking out a window. *How can it be?* Anita would have pinched herself except the pain in her leg was the stuff of nightmares, not dreams. Anita wondered about Mutti. *God, keep her safe and let me find her again.* So many others came to mind as they rolled through the dark countryside—Anita knew the farmlands were dotted with work camps and, even worse, death camps. She wondered if she'd ever see her *Tante* Käte or *Tante* Elsbeth or *Tante* Friede again. What about Wolfgang, Gerhard, and Rudi? Did Steffi make it to freedom? And was Pastor Hornig safe? Vati lived in Sorau. Was he, even now, fleeing from the Russians? Anita kept her face to the dark window so nobody could see the tears that rolled down onto her lap.

"Anita, wake up." Hella shook her. "We need to change trains here in Dresden."

As they stepped off the train, the air raid sirens began to wail, just like those days in Berlin. People ran every which way, screaming.

"The shelters!" Train personnel began to direct everyone to the shelters deep under the train station. "Head for the shelters!"

"Go, Hella!" Anita said. "I cannot make it down all those stairs with my leg."

"I'll help you."

The sirens continued to wail. "No, go!" Anita pushed Hella toward the stairs. "No matter what happens, I'm safe with God."

Hella was nearly pushed down the stairs by the masses of people. Anita put her hand to her mouth to send a pretend kiss in Hella's direction. Almost immediately she heard the first bomb scream through the air. The building shook with the concussion. Anita stumbled outside, thinking she stood a better chance out in the open than entombed in a building.

She remembered the words of the Lord, "I have put my words in your mouth and covered you with the shadow of my hand" as the bombs began to rain down on the city. The ground shuddered under the onslaught. The noise seared Anita's hearing and seemed to slice into her jaw. "Let me pass through the fire," she prayed, sending her words into the sky lit up by bombs.

The air seemed to whoosh as if all the oxygen had been sucked out of the world at once. The sky exploded in a firestorm of orange flame, and smoke rose in black columns to the heavens.

12
All Things Together

"Find a bed for this girl at once." The doctor called a nurse over to Anita. "I've rarely seen blood poisoning this bad. This young woman will likely lose her leg."

Anita cringed, remembering the almost-forgotten days when she danced on the stage of Century Hall in Breslau. Her leg—would she lose that now? She'd lost so much over the last twelve years. But the woman doctor had gentle hands and an encouraging smile. Anita trusted her immediately.

The doctor spoke to the nurse again, "Prep her for surgery so I can insert drainage tubes."

The nurse, Fräulein Grete, assisted Anita into a gown and helped her up on the bed. "What a shame," the nurse said. "A pretty blonde Aryan girl like yourself needs to be made whole again."

Uh-oh. Anita pretended to drift off into sleep rather than deal with the danger of the nurse discovering Anita's deception. Nazis still ran the hospital, of course, but most were

Nazi in name only—except her nurse, that is. Anita had seen many super-Nazis over the years and she recognized that fervor in Fräulein Grete. It signaled trouble.

After surviving the Dresden bombings and firestorm—more than 130,000 died that night—Anita had managed to find Hella. They eventually made their way to Bautzen. By that time, Anita's leg was so infected that Hella took her straight to the hospital. Anita's temperature registered 105 degrees when she arrived.

All she wanted to do was make her way to Czechoslovakia to find Mutti. Instead they rolled her into surgery. Fräulein Grete smoothed the younger girl's hair and smiled sympathetically as she put the ether mask on Anita's face.

A bright light overhead hurt Anita's eyes. *Where am I? Oh yes . . .* she reached under the covers and felt for her leg. *Thank You, God.* She still had two legs.

The kind doctor laughed a merry laugh. "I've heard of people talking under the influence of ether, but never like that little girl talked." The doctor shook her head. "She's been through more than the war . . ."

Fräulein Grete's face came into view. The woman's eyes narrowed and her top lip curled in hatred. "*Ja.* She talked all right." The nurse bumped hard against the bed, causing pain to shoot up Anita's foot into her leg.

From that moment, the nurse treated Anita cruelly and tried to make her miserable. Sometimes Anita heard Fräulein

Grete mouth *"Jude"* under her breath. She managed to convey that she'd be happy to let her patient die.

Fräulein Grete did her best to keep Anita's leg infected and to keep the doctor from finding out. She always managed to reroute the doctor around Anita's room, telling the doctor that Anita was nearly well. The nurse refused to change dressings or clean Anita's wound, and her condition worsened each day.

When Hella came to visit, she took one look at her friend; her temper spilled over; and she walked out of the room.

When she came back about an hour later, she had the doctor with her. Later, she told Anita what happened.

"I managed to find out where the doctor lived and walked all the way over there and knocked on her door."

"You didn't!" Anita put her hand over her mouth.

"I did. The doctor had obviously been sleeping." Hella smiled, "I said, 'My friend lies in your hospital dying because one of your nurses won't see that she gets proper care. You must help!' I told her you said she had been kind to you and helped you."

"Oh, Hella . . ."

"At first she seemed confused. She said that Fräulein Grete told her you were doing well and that she didn't need to look in on you anymore since the hospital was so overcrowded."

"Did she really?" Anita should have suspected this.

"The doctor got this angry look on her face and asked me to wait while she dressed."

From that time on, Fräulein Grete rarely came into Anita's room, but it still took four surgeries over many weeks to finally stem the infection in Anita's leg. Even at that, they still had drainage tubes coming out of her foot and thigh.

When she was finally able to get out of bed, Anita found she had to learn to walk all over again. Hella came in and spent hours helping her hobble up and down the aisles of the hospital.

One morning, as Anita pulled herself out of bed for a walk, the gauze bandage slipped. Hella saw ugly crisscrossing scars, raw skin, and open wounds. She gasped. "Why would God allow that to happen to you? You've always been faithful. How can you still believe He cares for you?"

Hella's anguished questions sounded like those being asked all over Germany. They always started, "How can a loving God permit . . ."

Anita took her friend's hand. "Hella, look. I still have my leg, don't I? That means I can walk all the way to Czechoslovakia if I need to."

"But if God could spare your leg, why didn't He spare all the scars and pain as well?" Hella sounded angry.

"I don't know. Many questions will never be answered until we get to heaven. Remember the verse we used to read at our Bible study in the barn in Barthold? Romans 8:28—remember? 'And we know that in all things God works for the good of those who love him, who have been called according to his purpose.'"

"Would you call this good?" Hella raised her eyebrows and gestured with her hand toward Anita's leg.

"But we haven't seen the 'working together' part yet. We have no idea how this fits into the whole plan. I don't doubt that it does, though."

She was still very weak several days later when they heard a familiar sound echoing through the hospital—*artillery.*

Without much warning, the staff moved patients into a cramped bomb shelter in preparation for a Russian invasion.

The frightening days turned into wakeful nights. Eight days passed while the Russians over ran the town. Anita had to share a bed with three other patients. The hospital staff did their best, but there was no food or medicine. Hunger battled with pain.

Nothing was as bad as fear. The Russians hated the Germans for what they'd done. The invading Russian army took town after town throughout Germany, and as they did, they destroyed property, tortured its citizens, and captured the soldiers, sending them on trains to Siberian prisoner-of-war camps.

When the Russian soldiers finally stormed the hospital shelter, everyone expected to die. The men were brutal. Elderly patients were thrown up against stone walls; men were beaten; women were abused. When two soldiers grabbed Anita, she shut her eyes and prayed. In the struggle, her gown pulled to the side, and the soldiers saw her leg with its angry wounds and oozing drains. One soldier gagged, and the other dropped her onto the floor. For the rest of the attack, they left her alone.

When they finally left, she silently thanked God that no one in the shelter had been killed. As frightening as the attack had been, she watched God's hand of protection and saw that "all things worked together" today in a way she could never have foreseen. The ugly wounds on her leg—those wounds Hella Frommelt hated—had saved her.

Others continued to suffer, and though Anita had been spared, she ached for them. She remembered Hella's question about why God allowed this kind of suffering. When someone asked the question, it always sounded as if God were responsible for the evil. But Anita knew wickedness was never God's choice. Anita looked around the room at the frightened patients, doctors, and nurses. She knew that God wept along with all of them.

When it was finally safe to come out of the air raid shelter, Anita hurried to her old bed, hoping to find the Bible that Pastor Hornig had given her all those years ago. How she had missed it those eight long days in the shelter!

It lay upside down on a table—soiled and crumpled. Many of the pages had been torn out. As Anita reluctantly put it in the dustbin, she couldn't help remembering Teddy— shabby, well-loved Teddy. Sometimes losing treasures hurt almost as much as losing people. *Auf Wiedersehen, Bible. Thank You, Lord, for letting me have it this long.*

The Russians had been pushed back temporarily, and the entire hospital was evacuated to Sudetenland, a safer place in the mountains between Germany and Czechoslovakia.

When Anita finally stepped out into the cold sunshine, she thanked God for healing her leg and caring for her throughout her long ordeal.

Now to find Mutti . . .

But the war raged on. Anita prayed amid the confusion. *Somehow, God, let me get to Theresienstadt and let Mutti be alive.* It wouldn't be easy. To the Russians, she looked like an Aryan. To the Czechs, her language made her suspect; and to the Germans, she'd always be a Jew.

The country was in shambles. Wherever Anita turned, she saw nothing more than piles of rubble and burned-out buildings. The war was as good as over, but the victors won no spoils—everything lay in ashes.

The people were in chaos. Hitler killed himself inside his Berlin bunker as the Russians raised the Red Flag over the city. The full extent of the Nazi evil unfolded little by little. The world reacted with horror. Everyone seemed to hate the Germans now, especially those people whose countries had been brutalized by the Nazis. Germans themselves recoiled from the *atrocities* committed under the *Swastika*. In the confusion, no one even bothered to sort out whether a German had been a Nazi or not.

Because people had been moved and resettled, it seemed like the whole country was trying to get home or trying to reunite with those who'd been lost or taken. Few homes remained unscathed. Travel was nearly impossible, and most of those trying to find family members had no money. They stayed at resettlement camps or Red Cross camps along the way.

As Anita traveled, she had nothing left but her old ski pants with deep pockets that went down to her knees, and a pajama top as a blouse. In those deep pockets, she carried some toilet paper, her ration card, a bit of a pencil, a pen, a broken comb, and Mutti's purse. Her leg still ached, and she walked with a limp, but she longed to get to Theresienstadt to see if anyone could tell her anything about Mutti.

Before she could go into Czechoslovakia, though, she needed to get a passport. She went to the passport office in Asch to apply. The man who helped her seemed worried.

"It's not safe for a German to travel into Czechoslovakia these days. The Czechs suffered terribly under Hitler and they hate the Germans."

"Still, I must go," Anita said. "I will trust God to protect me."

"Why must you go?"

"I must find my mother. They took her to Theresien-stadt." In response to his kind interest, she told him about Mutti and about Camp Barthold. She hadn't realized how much she told until she saw the pain on his face.

"Little Daughter," he said, "prepare yourself for the worst. Many of the prisoners who were not already sent to Auschwitz died in the typhoid epidemic that swept through the camp. When the Russians liberated it, prisoners were only one day away from finishing the construction of the gas chambers that would have exterminated them all." He shook his head in disbelief. He seemed to be talking more to himself than to her. "The Nazis tried to burn every piece of evidence before the Russians got there—including all the people."

Anita could not bear to hear more. She opened the purse left her by Mutti all those months ago and found just enough money to buy her passport and still have money left for train passage to Leitmeritz. The man carefully filled out all the information to issue the passport. When he handed it to her, it said "Victim of Nazism" on it.

Anita still understood the danger, so as she boarded the train, she decided to speak to no one. At each stop in Czecho-slovakia, more people got on the train. They laughed and talked and visited up and down the aisles. Anita feared someone would talk to her and hear that she spoke German. *Dear Lord, protect me.*

She woke suddenly to a hand on her shoulder. She flinched and turned to see who it was. A young man with curly dark hair smiled at her and began to talk to her in Czech.

She shook her head. His eyes grew dark and he asked in Czech if she was German. She shook her head again and handed the man her passport. He read it and put his head down on the back of her seat for a few minutes.

"I, too, am a Jew," he said in broken German as he slid into the seat next to her. "My name is Peter." He was returning from a concentration camp to try to find any family left in Prague, though he'd been told he was the only survivor.

They talked for a long time. Anita silently thanked the Lord for sending her someone to travel with her and speak for her.

When they arrived in Prague, he said he'd change trains and ride with her to Leitmeritz. He didn't mind waiting to see his burned-out home in Prague. When the train finally arrived, he helped Anita off the train and went over to talk to a policeman.

"I must say good-bye, now. I don't have much, but here are 150 *crowns* to help you."

"Thank you, Peter. I will pray for you."

His brown eyes crinkled in a smile of acknowledgment. "That policeman agreed to drive you the remaining distance to Theresienstadt. You will be safe, little friend."

"Auf Wiedersehen," Anita said as he left. *Auf Wiedersehen.*

The policeman drove Anita the eight harrowing kilometers to the gates of Theresienstadt. Debris littered the roads.

Bombs had wiped out whole portions. As they drove, the policeman used his broken German to warn her not to get her hopes up.

So much death—no wonder everyone gave warnings. Only a tiny fraction would ever see their loved ones again.

Theresienstadt came into view. As she looked at the massive stone walls of the fortress, she wondered what Mutti had thought as she was swallowed into the great *maws* of the prison.

As they got to the gates, she saw the skull and crossbones *quarantine* sign. Her stomach twisted. The policeman opened the car door anyway, and she got out and went up to the guard.

"Sorry, lady, we cannot allow anyone inside until the typhoid epidemic is officially declared over." The guard did look sorry.

Anita dropped her arms to her sides standing there in front of the guardhouse and wept silently. She had no words.

"Here, sit here," the guard said.

The policeman spoke up. "We understand the epidemic is over in every way except officially. Can't you let her in to find out her mother's fate? Keeping her out is too cruel. Truth—no matter how bad—is better than uncertainty."

"Thank you," she managed to mouth the words to the policeman.

The two guards stepped to the side and conferred together. When they came back, the first one said, "Go, then," He turned to the policeman. "Drive her inside to that white building. Let her get out by herself, and you turn around and leave."

The tears continued to stream down Anita's face. "Thank you."

As she got out of the car, she waved her thanks to her police friend. How many of these helpers had the Lord provided along the way? She'd never forget them.

Everything looked deserted inside the huge camp even though it was early afternoon. To look down the street on this balmy June day, it was hard to imagine the misery of the hundreds of thousands of people once imprisoned inside these walls. Anita somehow expected the evil to cling to the walls. Instead she saw a bird land on the packed dirt of the courtyard.

She limped up the steps to the main building just as the elderly woman in charge of this office arrived back from lunch. "I'm looking for my mother, Hilde Dittman."

Anita saw sympathy in the woman's eyes. She must have come in with the Red Cross when they took over the camp. "Dittman, Dittman." The woman opened a file drawer. "The name doesn't sound familiar." She looked through the list of survivors. "No, I don't see her here."

Anita silently prayed. *Please Lord; let me accept whatever may be. Let me remember that all things work together for Your purpose . . .*

"Please sit. I have one more place to check."

Anita sat down and waited. *How long has it been since Mutti was taken? It seems like forever, but if this is June 7th, it has only been eighteen months. It feels like years.* The time ticked away while the woman looked through files in another room. Five minutes. Ten minutes. Surely if she were here, they'd know it. *Lord, keep me from despair.*

143

The wide smile on the woman's face as she came back into the room said more than words could ever say. "Hilde Dittman is well. Here is her address. It is on the third floor, where she stays with three women."

Anita couldn't speak. She wrapped her arms around herself and sat hard on the bench, bent over, rocking with joy.

The woman smiled. She must not have enjoyed many happy scenes at her desk. "It says in the file that your mother turned down a bus ride back to Breslau because she wanted to wait in case you came. The buses left this morning. You would have missed her."

Thank You, Heavenly Father, for loving me and caring for me. Thank You for keeping Mutti safe. Thank You. Thank You. Anita remembered back to the days when she longed for Vati to acknowledge her. She'd now made her peace with Vati, but what she'd learned is that, no matter what her earthly father did, she always had a Heavenly Father who watched her every move.

Anita took the address and walked down the street. Outside the building she saw a woman coming down the stairs. "I am Anita Dittman. I'm looking for my mother. Do you—"

The woman put thin arms around Anita. "I feel I already know you, Anita. Your mother talks about you every day. Come . . . come!"

Anita followed up flights of stairs in the filthy building. She ignored the dull throb in her still healing leg. As the door opened, she saw a much thinner Mutti sitting in the old pink bathrobe Anita had left on the floor of the *synagogue* all those months ago.

"Mutti!" Anita rushed over to her mother and hugged her.

Mutti seemed stunned at first, but the tears puddled in her eyes. "*Mein Liebling*. You are safe. I prayed every day for God to keep you safe under the shadow of His hand."

"And God answered our prayers," said Anita.

Epilogue

The story of God's hand on Anita Dittman's life could fill volumes. This book tells part of the story. Other parts are told in her autobiography—*Trapped in Hitler's Hell* by Anita Dittman, as told to Jan Markell. Still other parts are told by Anita when she speaks. Many beloved people came into Anita's life during those dark days, and too many of them were lost in the Holocaust. But always, God covered Anita with the shadow of His hand.

Anita's sister, Hella, remained in England where she worked as a nurse, but at the end of the war, England could not take Anita and Mutti. The mother and daughter immigrated to America after living for nearly a year in a displaced persons camp. They eventually settled in Minnesota. Anita lives there still. After a career that included teaching, she now spends her time speaking to people about her experiences. Many have come to know the Lord through hearing of His presence in Anita's life.

In all, more than six million Jews died during Hitler's reign. Many Christians died as well for helping the Jews. Vati lived through the war and stayed in Germany until his death. Anita wrote to him, but she never returned to Germany. All three of Anita's aunts vanished. Steffi made it to freedom, as did her mother and Frau Wolf. Rudi, Wolfgang, and Gerhard Wolf, sadly, were captured and died after their escape attempt. Anita heard that Hella Frommelt lived. And Pastor Hornig lived through the war as well. He and the heroes at St. Barbara's selflessly cared for more Jews than will ever be counted.

When Anita speaks to groups of young people, they always ask if she ever tied on her ballet shoes and danced after the war. Her scarred leg healed, but she never went back to ballet. In her delicate German accent, she always says: "God has a very unique way of scooping up the shattered fragments of our hopes and dreams and molding them into a plan of His own—a plan vastly different from ours, but far more wonderful."

Glossary

Anti-Semitic. Prejudiced against Jewish people.

Artillery. Gunfire using larger guns.

Atrocities. Brutal torture and killing.

Auf Wiedersehen. The German words for good-bye.

Barre. A railing that is along a wall at waist height for ballet practice.

Bayonet; bayonets. Spears that fit on the end of guns.

Blacklisted; blacklisting. Added to the Gestapo's blacklist (a list of people they were planning to arrest).

Brownstone. A building built of reddish-brown stones.

Contagion. Diseases that are spread from person to person.

Crowns. Czechoslovakian money.

Danke. The German word for thank you.

Danseur. Male ballet dancer.

Der Führer. The German words for Hitler's title; The Leader.

Frau. The German word for Mrs.; Ms.

Fräulein. The German word for Miss.

Gestapo. Secret police.

Gott. The German word for God.

Heil. The German salute Nazis used for Hitler.

Herr. The German word for Mr.

Hitler Youth. A militaristic youth organization that taught Nazi ideas.

Ja. The German word for yes.

Jude; Juden. The German word for Jew; Jews.

Liebling. The German word for sweetheart.

Marks. Short for deutsche marks; German money.

Maws. Doors that are like jaws.

Mein. The German word for my.

Migs. Fighter airplanes.

Mutti. The German word for mom.

Nein. The German word for no.

Oma. The German word for grandma.

Parochial. Religious.

Quarantine. Where sick people who are contagious are kept away from others.

Reich. The German word for kingdom; empire.

Synagogue. A Jewish house of worship.

Tante. The German word for aunt.

Vati. The German word for dad.

Verboten. The German word for forbidden.

Wireless. Radio.

Wunderbar. The German word for wonderful.

DAUGHTERS OF THE FAITH

Young Harriet Tubman grew up in the early 1800's as a slave in Maryland. The story of her childhood is the story of God's faithfulness as He prepares her to eventually lead more than 300 people out of slavery through the Underground Railroad.

ISBN-13: 978-0-8024-4098-3

Olice Oatman and her sister are captured when their wagon train is raded by outlaw Yavapais. After enduring harsh treatment, they are ransomed by a band of Mohaves. She learns to see the Mohave design tattooed on her chin as a sign of God's love and deliverance.

ISBN-13: 978-0-8024-3638-2

In 1761 Phillis Wheatley was captured in Gambia and brought to America as a slave. She became the first African American to publish a book, and her writings would eventually win her freedom. But more importantly, her poetry still proclaims Christ.

ISBN-13: 978-0-8024-7639-5

A fascinating true-life story of 16-year-old Eliza Shirley who traveled from England to the United States to pioneer the work of the Salvation Army.

ISBN-13: 978-0-8024-4073-0

MOODY PUBLISHERS.

1-800-678-8812 · MOODYPUBLISHERS.COM

MORE DAUGHTERS OF THE FAITH

Based on the early life of Pocahontas, a young native girl who met and befriended a group of English settlers. When her tribe came into conflict with these new settlers, she offered her life to sve one of them.

ISBN-13: 978-0-8024-7640-1

The story of Mary, the daughter of John Bunyan, reveals a fierce determination for independence despite her blindness. But only when she admits she needs help does Mary tap into the Source of all strength.

ISBN-13: 978-0-8024-4099-0

Young Anita Dittman's world crumbles as Hitler begins his rise to power in Germany, but because she's a Christian and only half-Jewish, Anita feels sure she and her family are safe from "the Final Solution." She couldn't have been more wrong.

ISBN-13: 978-0-8024-4074-7

Mary Chilton was a young girl when she left her home in Holland and traveled to America on the Mayflower. Young readers will be enthralled with the trails, joys, and some surprises along her journey.

ISBN-13: 978-0-8024-3637-5

MOODY PUBLISHERS.

1-800-678-8812 · MOODYPUBLISHERS.COM